E. L. Doctorow's work ha
languages. His novels include
Times, The Book of Daniel, Ragtim
World's Fair, Billy Bathgate, The
Among his honours are the Na            Award, three
National Book Critics Circle awards, two PEN/Faulkner
awards, the Edith Wharton Citation for Fiction, the William
Dean Howells Medal of the American Academy of Arts and
Letters, and the presidentially conferred National Humanities
Medal. He lives in New York.

*Also by E. L. Doctorow*

Welcome to Hard Times

Big as Life

The Book of Daniel

Ragtime

Drinks Before Dinner (play)

Loon Lake

Lives of the Poets

World's Fair

Billy Bathgate

Jack London, Hemingway, and
the Constitution (essays)

The Waterworks

City of God

The March

# SWEET LAND
# STORIES

# SWEET LAND STORIES

## E. L. Doctorow

Abacus
An imprint of
Little, Brown Book Group
Brettenham House
Lancaster Place
London WC2E 7EN

A Member of the Hachette Livre Group of Companies

ABACUS

First published in the United States of America in 2004
by Random House, an imprint of The Random House Publishing Group,
a division of Random House, Inc
Published in paperback in the United States of America in 2005
by Random House Trade Paperbacks
First published in Great Britain in 2007 by Abacus

A CIP catalogue record for this book
is available from the British Library.

ISBN: 978-0-349-12019-5

The following stories were originally published in *The New Yorker*: 'A
House on the Plains' (June 18, 2001), 'Baby Wilson' (March 25, 2002),
'Jolene' (December 23, 2002, and December 30, 2002), and 'Walter
John Harmon' (May 12, 2003). Copyright © 2001, 2002, 2003 by
E. L. Doctorow

'Child, Dead, in the Rose Garden' was originally published in *The
Virginia Quarterly Review*, Spring 2004 issue. Copyright © 2004 by
E. L. Doctorow

Typeset in Baskerville by M Rules
Printed and bound in Great Britain by
Clays Ltd, St Ives plc

# CONTENTS

# A HOUSE ON THE PLAINS

Mama said I was thenceforth to be her nephew and to call her Aunt Dora. She said our fortune depended on her not having a son as old as eighteen who looked more like twenty. Say Aunt Dora, she said. I said it. She was not satisfied. She made me say it several times. She said I must say it believing she had taken me in since the death of her widowed brother, Horace. I said, I didn't know you had a brother named Horace. Of course I don't, she said with an amused glance at me. But it must be a good story if I could fool his son with it.

I was not offended as I watched her primp in the mirror, touching her hair as women do, although you can never see what afterwards is different.

With the life insurance, she had bought us a farm fifty miles west of the city line. Who would be there to care if I was her flesh and blood son or not? But she had her plans and was looking ahead. I had no plans. I had never had plans – just the inkling of something, sometimes, I didn't know what. I hunched over and went down the stairs with the second trunk wrapped to my back with a rope. Outside, at the foot of the stoop, the children were waiting with their scraped knees and socks around their ankles. They sang their own dirty words to a nursery rhyme. I shooed them away and they scattered off for a minute hooting and hollering and then of course came back again as I went up the stairs for the rest of the things.

Mama was standing at the empty bay window. While there is your court of inquest on the one hand, she said, on the other is your court of neighbors. Out in the country, she said, there will be no one to jump to conclusions. You can leave the door open, and the window shades up. Everything is clean and pure under the sun.

Well, I could understand that, but Chicago to my mind was the only place to be, with its grand hotels and its restaurants and paved avenues of trees and mansions. Of course not all Chicago was like that. Our third floor windows didn't look out on much besides the row of boardinghouses across the street. And it is true that in the summer people of refinement could be overcome with the smell of the stockyards, although it didn't bother me. Winter was another complaint that wasn't mine. I never minded the cold. The wind in winter blowing off the lake went whipping the ladies' skirts like a demon dancing around their ankles. And winter or summer you could always ride the electric streetcars if you had nothing else to do. I above all liked the city because it was filled with people all a-bustle, and the clatter of hooves and carriages, and with delivery wagons and drays and the peddlers and the boom and clank of the freight trains. And when those black clouds came sailing in from the west, pouring thunderstorms upon us so that you couldn't hear the cries or curses of humankind, I liked that best of all. Chicago could stand up under the worst God had to offer. I understood why it was built – a place for trade, of course, with railroads and ships and so on, but mostly to give all of us a magnitude of defiance that is not provided by one house on the plains. And the plains is where those storms come from.

Besides, I would miss my friend Winifred Czerwinska, who stood now on her landing as I was going downstairs with the suitcases. Come in a minute, she said, I want to give you something. I went in and she closed the door behind me. You can put those down, she said of the suitcases.

My heart always beat faster in Winifred's presence. I could feel it and she knew it too and it made her happy. She put her hand on my chest now and she stood on tiptoes to kiss me with her hand under my shirt feeling my heart pump.

Look at him, all turned out in a coat and tie. Oh, she said, with her eyes tearing up, what am I going to do without my Earle? But she was smiling.

Winifred was not a Mama type of woman. She was a slight, skinny thing, and when she went down the stairs it was like a bird hopping. She wore no powder or perfumery except by accident the confectionary sugar which she brought home on her from the bakery where she worked behind the counter. She had sweet, cool lips but one eyelid didn't come up all the way over the blue, which made her not as pretty as she might otherwise be. And of course she had no titties to speak of.

You can write me a letter or two and I will write back, I said.

What will you say in your letter?

I will think of something, I said.

She pulled me into the kitchen, where she spread her feet and put her forearms flat on a chair so that I could raise her frock and fuck into her in the way she preferred. It didn't take that long, but even so, while Winifred wiggled and made her little cat sounds I could hear Mama calling from upstairs as to where I had gotten.

We had ordered a carriage to take us and the luggage at the same time rather than sending it off by the less expensive Railway Express and taking a horsecar to the station. That was not my idea, but exactly the amounts that were left after Mama bought the house only she knew. She came down the steps under her broad-brim hat and widow's veil and held her skirts at her shoe tops as the driver helped her into the carriage.

We were making a grand exit in full daylight. This was pure Mama as she lifted her veil and glanced with contempt at the neighbors looking out from their windows. As for the nasty children, they had gone quite quiet at our display of elegance. I swung up beside her and closed the door and at her instruction threw a handful of pennies on the sidewalk, and I watched the children push and shove one another and dive to their knees as we drove off.

When we had turned the corner, Mama opened the hatbox I had put on the seat. She removed her black hat and replaced it with a blue number trimmed in fake flowers. Over her mourning dress she draped a glittery shawl in striped colors like the rainbow. There, she said. I feel so much better now. Are you all right, Earle?

Yes, Mama, I said.

Aunt Dora.

Yes, Aunt Dora.

I wish you had a better mind, Earle. You could have paid more attention to the Doctor when he was alive. We had our disagreements, but he was smart for a man.

The train stop of La Ville was a concrete platform and a lean-to for a waiting room and no ticket-agent window. When you got off, you were looking down an alley to a glimpse of their Main Street. Main Street had a feed store, a post office, a white wooden church, a granite stone bank, a haberdasher, a town square with a four-story hotel, and in the middle of the square on the grass the statue of a Union soldier. It could all be counted because there was just one of everything. A man with a dray was willing to take us. He drove past a few other streets where first there were some homes of substance and another church or two but then, as you moved further out from the town center, worn looking one-story shingle houses with dark little porches and garden plots

7

and clotheslines out back with only alleys separating them. I couldn't see how, but Mama said there was a population of over three thousand living here. And then after a couple of miles through farmland, with a silo here and there off a straight road leading due west through fields of corn, there swung into view what I had not expected, a three-story house of red brick with a flat roof and stone steps up to the front door like something just lifted out of a street of row houses in Chicago. I couldn't believe anyone had built such a thing for a farmhouse. The sun flared in the windowpanes and I had to shade my eyes to make sure I was seeing what I saw. But that was it in truth, our new home.

Not that I had the time to reflect, not with Mama settling in. We went to work. The house was cobwebbed and dusty and it was rank with the droppings of animal life. Blackbirds were roosting in the top floor, where I was to live. Much needed to be done, but before long she had it all organized and a parade of wagons was coming from town with the furniture she'd Expressed and no shortage of men willing to hire on for a day with hopes for more from this grand good-looking lady with the rings on several fingers. And so the fence went up for the chicken yard, and the weed fields beyond were being plowed under and the watering hole for stock was dredged and a new privy was dug, and I thought for some days Mama was the biggest employer of La Ville, Illinois.

But who would haul the well water and wash the clothes and bake the bread? A farm was a different life, and days went by when I slept under the roof of the third floor and felt the heat of the day still on my pallet as I looked through the little window at the remoteness of the stars and I felt unprotected as I never had in the civilization we had retreated from. Yes, I thought, we had moved backward from the world's progress, and for the first time I wondered about Mama's judgment. In all our travels from state to state and with all the various obstacles to her ambition, I had never thought to question it. But no more than this house was a farmer's house was she a farmer, and neither was I.

One evening we stood on the front steps watching the sun go down behind the low hills miles away.

Aunt Dora, I said, what are we up to here?

I know, Earle. But some things take time.

She saw me looking at her hands, how red they had gotten.

I am bringing an immigrant woman down from Wisconsin. She will sleep in that room behind the kitchen. She's to be here in a week or so.

Why? I said. There's women in La Ville, the wives of all these locals come out here for a day's work who could surely use the money.

I will not have some woman in the house who will only take back to town what she sees and hears. Use what sense God gave you, Earle.

I am trying, Mama.

Aunt Dora, goddamnit.

Aunt Dora.

Yes, she said. Especially here in the middle of nowhere and with nobody else in sight.

She had tied her thick hair behind her neck against the heat and she went about now loose in a smock without her usual women's underpinnings.

But doesn't the air smell sweet, she said. I'm going to have a screen porch built and fit it out with a settee and some rockers so we can watch the grand show of nature in comfort.

She ruffled my hair. And you don't have to pout, she said. You may not appreciate it here this moment with the air so peaceful and the birds singing and nothing much going on in any direction you can see. But we're still in business, Earle. You can trust me on that.

And so I was assured.


By and by we acquired an old-fashioned horse and buggy to take us to La Ville and back when Aunt Dora had to go to the bank or the post office or provisions were needed. I was the driver and horse groom. He – the horse – and I did not get along. I wouldn't give him a name. He was ugly, with a sway back and legs that trotted out splayed. I had butchered and trimmed better looking plugs than this in Chicago. Once, in the barn, when I was putting him up for the night, he took a chomp in the air just off my shoulder.

Another problem was Bent, the handyman Mama had hired for the steady work. No sooner did she begin taking him upstairs of an afternoon than he was strutting around like he owned the place. This was a problem as I saw it. Sure enough, one day he told me to do something. It was one of his own chores. I thought you was the hired one, I said to him. He was ugly, like a relation of the horse – he was shorter than you thought he ought to be with his long arms and big gnarled hands hanging from them.

Get on with it, I said.

Leering, he grabbed me by the shoulder and put his mouth up to my ear. I seen it all, he said. Oh yes. I seen everything a man could wish to see.

At this I found myself constructing a fate for Bent the handyman. But he was so drunkly stupid I knew Mama must have her own plan for him or else why would she play up to someone of this ilk, and so I held my ideas in abeyance.

In fact I was by now thinking I could wrest some hope from the wide loneliness of this farm with views of the plains as far as you could see. What had come to mind? A sense of expectancy that I recognized from times past. Yes. I had sensed that whatever was going to happen had begun. There was not only the handyman. There were the orphan children. She had contracted for three from the do-good agency in New York that took orphans off the streets and washed and dressed them and put them on the train to their foster homes in the midland. Ours were comely enough children, though pale, two boys and a girl with papers that gave their ages, six, six, and eight, and as I trotted them to the farm they sat up behind me staring at the countryside without a word. And so now they were installed in the back bedroom on the second floor, and they were not like the miserable street rats from our neighborhood in the city. These were quiet children except for the weeping they were sometimes given to at night, and by and large they did as they were told. Mama had some real feeling for them – Joseph and Calvin and the girl, Sophie, in particular. There were no conditions as to what faith they were to be brought up in nor did we have any in mind. But on Sundays, Mama took to showing them off to the Methodist church in La Ville in the new clothes she had bought for them. It gave her pleasure, and was besides a presentation of her own pride of position in life. Because it turned out, as I was learning, that even in the farthest reaches of the countryside, you lived in society.

And in this great scheme of things my Aunt Dora required little Joseph, Calvin, and Sophie to think of her as their mama. Say Mama, she said to them. And they said it.

Well, so here was this household of us, ready made, as something bought from a department store. Fannie was the imported cook and housekeeper, who by Mama's design spoke no English but understood well enough what had to be done. She was heavyset, like Mama, with the strength to work hard. And besides Bent, who skulked about by the barns and fences in the sly pretense of work, there was a real farmer out beyond, who was sharecropping the acreage in corn. And two mornings a week a retired county teacher woman came by to tutor the children in reading and arithmetic.

Mama said one evening: We are an honest to goodness enterprise here, a functioning family better off than most in these parts, but we are running at a deficit, and if we don't have something in hand before winter the only resources will be the insurance I took out on the little ones.

She lit the kerosene lamp on the desk in the parlor and wrote out a Personal and read it to me: "Widow offering partnership in prime farmland to dependable man. A modest investment is required." What do you think, Earle?

It's okay.

She read it again to herself. No, she said. It's not good enough. You've got to get them up off their ass and out of the house to the Credit Union and then on a train to La Ville, Illinois. That's a lot to do with just a few words. How about this: "Wanted!" That's good, it bespeaks urgency. And doesn't every male in the world thinks he's what is wanted? "Wanted – Recently widowed woman with bountiful farm in God's own country has need of Nordic man of sufficient means for partnership in same."

What is Nordic? I said.

Well that's pure cunning right there, Earle, because that's all they got in the states where we run this – Swedes and Norwegies just off the boat. But I'm letting them know a lady's preference.

All right, but what's that you say there – "of sufficient means"? What Norwegie off the boat'll know what that's all about?

This gave her pause. Good for you, Earle, you surprise me sometimes. She licked the pencil point. So we'll just say "with cash."

We placed the Personal in one paper at a time in towns in Minnesota, and then in South Dakota. The letters of courtship commenced, and Mama kept a ledger with the names and dates of arrival, making sure to give each candidate his sufficient time. We always advised the early-morning train when the town was not yet up and about. Beside my regular duties, I had to take part in the family reception. They would be welcomed into the parlor, and Mama would serve coffee from a wheeled tray, and Joseph, Calvin, and Sophie, her children, and I, her nephew, would sit on the sofa and hear our biographies conclude with a happy ending, which was the present moment. Mama was so well spoken at these times I was as apt as the poor foreigners to be caught up in her modesty, so seemingly unconscious was she of the great-heartedness of her. They by and large did not see through to her self-congratulation. And of course she was a large, handsome woman to look at. She wore her simple finery for these first impressions, a plain pleated gray cotton skirt and a starched white shirtwaist and no jewelry but the gold cross on a chain that fell between her bosoms and her hair combed upward and piled atop her head in a state of fetching carelessness.

I am their dream of heaven on earth, Mama said to me

along about the third or fourth. Just to see how their eyes light up standing beside me looking out over their new land. Puffing on their pipes, giving me a glance that imagines me as available for marriage – who can say I don't give value in return?

Well that is one way to look at it, I said.

Don't be smug, Earle. You're in no position. Tell me an easier way to God's blessed Heaven than a launch from His Heaven on earth. I don't know of one.

And so our account in the La Ville Savings Bank began to compound nicely. The late summer rain did just the right thing for the corn, as even I could see, and it was an added few unanticipated dollars we received from the harvest. If there were any complications to worry about it was that fool Bent. He was so dumb he was dangerous. At first Mama indulged his jealousy. I could hear them arguing upstairs – he roaring away and she assuring him so quietly I could hardly hear what she said. But it didn't do any good. When one of the Norwegies arrived, Bent just happened to be in the yard, where he could have a good look. One time there was his ugly face peering through the porch window. Mama signaled me with a slight motion of her head and I quickly got up and pulled the shade.

It was true Mama might lay it on a bit thick. She might coquette with this one, yes, just as she might affect a widow's piety with that one. It all depended on her instinct of the particular man's character. It was easy enough to make believers of them. If I had to judge them as a whole I would say they were simple men, not exactly stupid, but lacking command of our language and with no wiles of their own. By whatever combination of sentiments and signatures, she never had anything personal intended but the business at hand, the step-by-step encouragement of the cash into our bank account.

The fool Bent imagined Mama looking for a husband from among these men. His pride of possession was offended. When he came to work each morning, he was often three sheets to the wind and if she happened not to invite him upstairs for the afternoon siesta, he would go home in a state, turning at the road to shake his fist and shout up at the windows before he set out for town in his crouching stride.

Mama said to me on one occasion, The damned fool has feelings.

Well that had not occurred to me in the way she meant it, and maybe in that moment my opinion of the handyman was raised to a degree. Not that he was any less dangerous. Clearly he had never learned that the purpose of life is to improve your station in it. It was not an idea available to him. Whatever you were, that's what you would always be. So he saw these foreigners who couldn't even talk right not only as usurpers but as casting a poor light on his existence. Was I in his position, I would learn from the example of these immigrants and think what I could do to put together a few dollars and buy some farm-land for myself. Any normal person would think that. Not him. He just got enough of the idea through his thick skull to realize he lacked the hopes of even the lowest foreigner. So I would come back from the station with one of them in the buggy and the fellow would step down, his plaid suit and four-in-hand and his bowler proposing him as a man of sufficient means, and it was like a shadow and sudden chilling as from a black cloud came over poor Bent, who could understand only that it was too late for him – everything, I mean, it was all too late.

And finally, to show how dumb he was, what he didn't realize was that it was all too late for them, too.

Then everything green began to fade off yellow, the summer rains were gone, and the wind off the prairie blew the dried-out topsoil into gusty swirls that rose and fell like waves in a dirt sea. At night the windows rattled. At first frost, the two little boys caught the croup.

Mama pulled the Wanted ad back from the out-of-state papers, saying she needed to catch her breath. I didn't know what was in the ledger, but her saying that meant our financial situation was improved. And now, as with all farm families, winter would be a time for rest.

Not that I was looking forward to it. How could I with nothing to do?

I wrote a letter to my friend Winifred Czerwinska, in Chicago. I had been so busy until now I hardly had the time to be lonely. I said that I missed her and hoped before too long to come back to city life. As I wrote, a rush of pity for myself came over me and I almost sobbed at the picture in my mind of the Elevated trains and the moving lights of the theater marquees and the sounds I imagined of the streetcars and even of the lowings of the abattoir where I had earned my wages. But I only said I hoped she would write me back.

I think the children felt the same way about this cold countryside. They had been displaced from a greater distance away, in a city larger than Chicago. They could not have been colder huddled at some steam grate than they were now with blankets to their chins. From the day they arrived they wouldn't leave one another's side, and though she was not croupy herself, Sophie stayed with the two boys in their bedroom, attending to their hackings and wheezes and sleeping in an armchair in the night. Fannie cooked up oatmeal for their breakfasts and soup for their dinners, and I took it upon myself to bring the tray upstairs in order to get them talking to me, since we were all related in a sense and in their minds I would be an older boy orphan taken in, like them. But they would not talk much, only answering my friendly questions yes or no in their soft voices, looking at me all the while with some dark expectation in their eyes. I didn't like that. I knew they talked among themselves all the time. These were streetwise children who had quickly apprised themselves of the lay of the land. For instance, they knew enough to stay out of Bent's way when he was drinking. But when he was sober they followed him around. And one day I had gone into the stable, to harness the horse, and found them snooping around in there, so they were not without unhealthy curiosity. Then there was the unfortunate matter of one of the boys, Joseph, the shorter darker one – he had found a pocket watch and watch fob in the yard, and when I said it was mine he said it wasn't. Whose is it then, I said. I know it's not yours, he said as he finally handed it over. To make more of an issue of it was not wise, so I didn't, but I hadn't forgotten.

Mama and I were nothing if not prudent, discreet, and in full consideration of the feelings of others in all our ways and means, but I believe children have a sense that enables them to know something even when they can't say what it is. As a child I must have had it, but of course it leaves you as you grow up. It may be a trait children are given so that they will survive long enough to grow up.

But I didn't want to think the worst. I reasoned to myself that were I plunked down so far away from my streets among strangers who I was ordered to live with as their relation, in the middle of this flat land of vast empty fields that would stir in any breast nothing but a recognition of the presiding deafness and dumbness of the natural world, I too would behave as these children were behaving.


And then one stinging cold day in December, I had gone into town to pick up a package from the post office. We had to write away to Chicago for those things it would not do to order from the local merchants. The package was in, but also a letter addressed to me, and it was from my friend Winifred Czerwinska.

Winifred's penmanship made me smile. The letters were thin and scrawny and did not keep to a straight line but went slanting in a downward direction, as if some of her mortal being was transferred to the letter paper. And I knew she had written from the bakery, because there was some powdered sugar in the folds.

She was so glad to hear from me and to know where I was. She thought I had forgotten her. She said she missed me. She said she was bored with her job. She had saved her money and hinted that she would be glad to spend it on something interesting, like a train ticket. My ears got hot reading that. In my mind I saw Winifred squinting up at me. I could almost feel her putting her hand under my shirt to feel my heart the way she liked to do.

But on the second page she said maybe I would be interested in news from the old neighborhood. There was going to be another inquest, or maybe the same one reopened.

It took me a moment to understand she was talking about the Doctor, Mama's husband in Chicago. The Doctor's relatives had asked for his body to be dug up. Winifred found this out from the constable who knocked on her door as he was doing with everyone. The police were trying to find out where we had gone, Mama and I.

I hadn't gotten your letter yet, Winifred said, so I didn't have to lie about not knowing where you were.

I raced home. Why did Winifred think she would otherwise have to lie? Did she believe all the bad gossip about us? Was she like the rest of them? I thought she was different. I was disappointed in her, and then I was suddenly very mad at Winifred.

Mama read the letter differently. Your Miss Czerwinska is our friend, Earle. That's something higher than a lover. If I have worried about her slow eye being passed on to the children, if it shows up we will just have to have it corrected with surgery.

What children, I said.

The children of your blessed union with Miss Czerwinska, Mama said.

Do not think Mama said this merely to keep me from worrying about the Chicago problem. She sees things before other people see them. She has plans going out through all directions of the universe – she is not a one-track mind, my Aunt Dora. I was excited by her intentions for me, as if I had thought of them myself. Perhaps I had thought of them myself as my secret, but she had read my secret and was now giving her approval. Because I certainly did like Winifred Czerwinska, whose lips tasted of baked goods and who loved it so when I fucked into her. And now it was all out in the open, and Mama not only knew my feelings but expressed them for me and it only remained for the young lady to be told that we were engaged.

I thought then her visiting us would be appropriate, especially as she was prepared to pay her own way. But Mama said, Not yet, Earle. Everyone in the house knew you were loving her up, and if she was to quit her job in the bakery and pack a bag and go down to the train station, even the Chicago police, as stupid as they are, they would put two and two together.

Of course I did not argue the point, though I was of the opinion that the police would find out where we were regardless. There were indications all over the place – not anything as difficult as a clue to be discerned only by the smartest of detectives, but bank account transfers, forwarding mail, and such. Why, even the driver who took us to the station might have picked up some remark of ours, and certainly a ticket-seller at Union Station might remember us. Mama being such an unusual-looking woman, very decorative and regal to the male eye, she would surely be remembered by a ticket-seller, who would not see her like from one year to the next.

Maybe a week went by before Mama expressed an opinion about the problem. You can't trust people, she said. It's that damn sister of his, who didn't even shed a tear at the grave. Why, she even told me how lucky the Doctor was to have found me so late in life.

I remember, I said.

And how I had taken such good care of him.

Which was true, I said.

Relatives are the fly in the ointment, Earle.


Mama's not being concerned so much as she was put out meant to me that we had more time than I would have thought. Our quiet lives of winter went on as before, though as I watched and waited she was obviously thinking things through. I was satisfied to wait, even though she was particularly attentive to Bent, inviting him in for dinner as if he was not some hired hand but a neighboring farmer. And I had to sit across the table on the children's side and watch him struggle to hold the silver in his fist and slurp his soup and pity him the way he had pathetically combed his hair down and tucked his shirt in and the way he folded his fingers under when he happened to see the dirt under his nails. This is good eats, he said aloud to no one in particular, and even Fannie, as she served, gave a little hmph as if despite having no English she understood clearly enough how out of place he was here at our table.

Well as it turned out there were things I didn't know, for instance that the little girl, Sophie, had adopted Bent, or maybe made a pet of him as you would any dumb beast, but they had become friends of a sort and she had confided to him remarks she overheard in the household. Maybe if she was making Mama into her mama she thought she was supposed to make the wretched bum of a hired hand into her father, I don't know. Anyway, there was this alliance between them that showed to me that she would never rise above her unsavory life in the street as a vagrant child. She looked like an angel with her little bow mouth and her pale face and gray eyes and her hair in a single long braid, which Mama herself did every morning, but she had the hearing of a bat and could stand on the second-floor landing and listen all the way down the stairs to our private conversations in the front parlor. Of course I only knew that later. It was Mama who learned that Bent was putting it about to his drinking cronies in town that the Madame Dora they thought was such a lady was his love slave and a woman on the wrong side of the law back in Chicago.

Mama, I said, I have never liked this fool, though I have been holding my ideas in abeyance for the fate I have in mind for him. But here he accepts our wages and eats our food then goes and does this?

Hush, Earle, not yet, not yet, she said. But you are a good son to me, and I can take pride that as a woman alone I have bred in you the highest sense of family honor. She saw how troubled I was. She hugged me. Are you not my very own knight of the roundtable? she said. But I was not comforted. It seemed to me that forces were massing slowly but surely against us in a most menacing way. I didn't like it. I didn't like it that we were going along as if everything was hunky dory, even to giving a grand Christmas Eve party for the several people in La Ville who Mama had come to know – how they all drove out in their carriages under the moon that was so bright on the plains of snow that it was like a black daytime, the local banker, the merchants, the pastor of the First Methodist church, and other such dignitaries and their wives. The spruce tree in the parlor was imported from Minnesota and all alight with candles and the three children were dressed for the occasion and went around with cups of eggnog for the assembled guests. I knew how important it was for Mama to establish her reputation as a person of class who had flattered the community by joining it, but all these people made me nervous. I didn't think it was wise having so many rigs parked in the yard and so many feet tromping about the house or going out to the privy. Of course it was a lack of self-confidence on my part, and how often was it Mama had warned me nothing was more dangerous than that, because it was translated into the face and physique as wrongdoing, or at least defenselessness, which amounted to the same thing. But I couldn't help it. I remembered the pocket watch that the little sniveling Joseph had found and held up to me swinging it from its fob. I sometimes made mistakes, I was human, and who knew what other mistakes lay about for someone to find and hold up to me.

But now Mama looked at me over the heads of her guests. The children's tutor had brought her harmonium and we all gathered around the fireplace for some carol singing. Given Mama's look, I sang the loudest. I have a good tenor voice and I sent it aloft to turn heads and make the La Villers smile. I imagined decking the halls with boughs of holly until there was kindling and brush enough to set the whole place ablaze.


Just after the New Year a man appeared at our door, another Swede, with his Gladstone bag in his hand. We had not run the Wanted ad all winter and Mama was not going to be home to him, but this fellow was the brother of one of them who had responded to it the previous fall. He gave his name, Henry Lundgren, and said his brother Per Lundgren had not been heard from since leaving Wisconsin to look into the prospect here.

Mama invited him in and sat him down and had Fannie bring in some tea. The minute I looked at him, I remembered the brother. Per Lundgren had been all business. He did not blush or go shy in Mama's presence, nor did he ogle. Instead, he asked sound questions. He had also turned the conversation away from his own circumstances, family relations and so on, which Mama put people through in order to learn who was back home and might be waiting. Most of the immigrants, if they had family, it was still in the old country, but you had to make sure. Per Lundgren was close mouthed, but he did admit to being unmarried and so we decided to go ahead.

And here was Henry, the brother he had never mentioned, sitting stiffly in the wing chair with his arms folded and the aggrieved expression on his face. They had the same reddish fair skin, with a long jaw and thinning blond hair, and pale woeful-looking eyes with blond eyelashes. I would say Henry here was the younger by a couple of years, but he turned out to be as smart as Per, or maybe even smarter. He did not seem to be as convinced of the sincerity of Mama's expressions of concern as I would have liked. He said his brother had made the trip to La Ville with other stops planned afterwards to two more business prospects, a farm some twenty miles west of us and another in Indiana. Henry had traveled to these places, which is how he learned that his brother never

26

arrived for his appointments. He said Per had been traveling with something over two thousand dollars in his money belt.

My goodness, that is a lot of money, Mama said.

Our two savings, Henry said. He comes here to see your farm. I have the advertisement, he said pulling a piece of newspaper from his pocket. This is the first place he comes to see.

I'm not sure he ever arrived, Mama said. We've had many inquiries.

He arrived, Henry Lundgren said. He arrived the night before so he will be on time the next morning. This is my brother. It is important to him, even if it costs money. He sleeps at the hotel in La Ville.

How could you know that? Mama said.

I know from the guest book in the La Ville hotel where I find his signature, Henry Lundgren said.

Mama said, All right, Earle, we've got a lot more work to do before we get out of here.

We're leaving?

What is today, Monday. I want to be on the road Thursday the latest. I thought with the inquest matter back there we were okay at least to the spring. This business of a brother pushes things up a bit.

I am ready to leave.

I know you are. You have not enjoyed the farm life, have you? If that Swede had told us he had a brother, he wouldn't be where he is today. Too smart for his own good, he was. Where is Bent?

She went out to the yard. He was standing at the corner of the barn peeing a hole in the snow. She told him to take the carriage and go to La Ville and pick up a half a dozen gallon cans of kerosene at the hardware. They were to be put on our credit.

It occurred to me that we still had a goodly amount of our winter supply of kerosene. I said nothing. Mama had gone into action, and I knew from experience that every-thing would come clear by and by.

And then late that night, when I was in the basement, she called downstairs to me that Bent was coming down to help.

I don't need help, thank you, Aunt Dora, I said, so astonished that my throat went dry.

At that they both clomped down the stairs and back to the potato bin where I was working. Bent was grinning that toothy grin of his as always, to remind me he had cer-tain privileges.

Show him, Mama said to me. Go ahead, it's all right, she assured me.

So I did, I showed him. I showed him something to hand. I opened the top of the gunnysack and he looked down it.

The fool's grin disappeared, the unshaven face went pale, and he started to breathe through his mouth. He gasped, he couldn't catch his breath, a weak cry came from him, and he looked at me in my rubber apron and his knees buckled and he fainted dead away.

Mama and I stood over him. Now he knows, I said. He will tell them.

Maybe, Mama said, but I don't think so. He's now one of us. We have just made him an accessory.

An accessory?

After the fact. But he'll be more than that by the time I get through with him, she said.

We threw some water on him and lifted him to his feet. Mama took him up to the kitchen and gave him a couple of quick swigs. Bent was thoroughly cowed, and when I came upstairs and told him to follow me, he jumped out of his chair as if shot. I handed him the gunnysack. It was not that heavy for someone like him. He held it in one hand at arm's length as if it would bite. I led him to the old dried up well behind the house, where he dropped it down into the muck. I poured the quicklime in and then we lowered some rocks down and nailed the well cover back on, and Bent the handyman he never said a word but just stood there shivering and waiting for me to tell him what to do next.

Mama had thought of everything. She had paid cash down for the farm but somewhere or other got the La Ville bank to give her a mortgage and so when the house burned, it was the bank's money. She had been withdrawing from the account all winter, and now that we were closing shop, she mentioned me the actual sum of our wealth for the first time. I was very moved to be confided in, like her partner.

But really it was the small touches that showed her genius. For instance, she had noted immediately of the inquiring brother Henry that he was in height not much taller than I am. Just as in Fannie the housekeeper she had hired a woman of a girth similar to her own. Meanwhile, at her instruction, I was letting my dark beard grow out. And at the end, before she had Bent go up and down the stairs pouring the kerosene in every room, she made sure he was good and drunk. He would sleep through the whole thing in the stable, and that's where they found him with his arms wrapped like a lover's arms around an empty can of kerosene.

The plan was for me to stay behind for a few days just to keep an eye on things. We have pulled off something prodigious that will go down in the books, Mama said. But that means all sorts of people will be flocking here and you can never tell when the unexpected arises. Of course everything will be fine, but if there's something more we have to do you will know it.

Yes, Aunt Dora.

Aunt Dora was just for here, Earle.

Yes, Mama.

Of course, even if there was no need to keep an eye out you would still have to wait for Miss Czerwinska.

This is where I didn't understand her thinking. The one bad thing in all of this is that Winifred would read the news in the Chicago papers. There was no safe way I could get in touch with her now that I was dead. That was it, that was the end of it. But Mama had said it wasn't necessary to get in touch with Winifred. This remark made me angry.

You said you liked her, I said.

I do, Mama said.

You called her our friend, I said.

She is.

I know it can't be helped, but I wanted to marry Winifred Czerwinska. What can she do now but dry her tears and maybe light a candle for me and go out and find herself another boyfriend.

Oh, Earle, Earle, Mama said, you know nothing about a woman's heart.

But anyhow, I followed the plan to stay on a few days and it wasn't that hard with a dark stubble and a different hat and a long coat. There were such crowds nobody would notice anything that wasn't what they'd come to see, that's what a fever was in these souls. Everyone was streaming down the road to see the tragedy. They were in their carriages and they were walking and standing up in drays – people were paying for anything with wheels to get them out there from town – and after the newspapers ran the story, they were coming not just from La Ville and the neighboring farms but from out of state in their automobiles and on the train from Indianapolis and Chicago. And with the crowds came the hawkers to sell sandwiches and hot coffee, and peddlers with balloons and little flags and whirligigs for the children. Someone had taken photographs of the laid out skeletons in their crusts of burlap and printed them up as postcards for mailing, and these were going like hotcakes.

The police had been inspired by the charred remains they found in the basement to look down the well and then to dig up the chicken yard and the floor of the stable. They had brought around a rowboat to dredge the water hole. They were really very thorough. They kept making their discoveries and laying out what they found in neat rows inside the barn. They had called in the county sheriff and his men to help with the crowds and they got some kind of order going, keeping people in lines to pass them by the open barn doors so everyone would have a turn. It was the only choice the police had if they didn't want a riot, but even then the oglers went around back all the way up the road to get into the procession again – it was the two headless remains of Madame Dora and her nephew that drew the most attention, and of course the wrapped bundles of the little ones.

There was such heat from this population that the snow was gone from the ground and on the road and in the yard and behind the house and even into the fields where the trucks and automobiles were parked everything had turned to mud so that it seemed even the season was transformed. I just stood and watched and took it all in, and it was amazing to see so many people with this happy feeling of spring, as if a population of creatures had formed up out of the mud especially for the occasion. That didn't help the smell any, though no one seemed to notice. The house itself made me sad to look at, a smoking ruin that you could see the sky through. I had become fond of that house. A piece of the floor hung down from the third story where I had my room. I disapproved of people pulling off the loose brickwork to take home for a souvenir. There was a lot of laughing and shouting, but of course I did not say anything. In fact I was able to rummage around the ruin without drawing attention to myself, and sure enough I found something – it was the syringe for which I knew Mama would be thankful.

I overheard some conversation about Mama – what a terrible end for such a fine lady who loved children was the gist of it. I thought as time went on, in the history of our life of La Ville, I myself would not be remembered very clearly. Mama would become famous in the papers as a tragic victim mourned for her good works whereas I would only be noted down as a dead nephew. Even if the past caught up with her reputation and she was slandered as the suspect widow of several insured husbands, I would still be in the shadows. This seemed to me an unjust outcome considering the contribution I had made, and I found myself for a moment resentful. Who was I going to be in life now that I was dead and not even Winifred Czerwinska was there to bend over for me.

Back in town at night, I went behind the jail to the cell window where Bent was and I stood on a box and called to him softly, and when his bleary face appeared, I ducked to the side where he couldn't see me and I whispered these words: "Now you've seen it all, Bent. Now you have seen everything."

I stayed in town to meet every train that came through from Chicago. I could do that without fear – there was such a heavy traffic all around, such swirls of people, all of them too excited and thrilled to take notice of someone standing quietly in a doorway or sitting on the curb in the alley behind the station. And as Mama told me, I knew nothing about the heart of a woman, because all at once there was Winifred Czerwinska stepping down from the coach, her suitcase in her hand. I lost her for a moment through the steam from the locomotive blowing across the platform, but then there she was in her dark coat and a little hat and the most forlorn expression I have ever seen on a human being. I waited till the other people had drifted away before I approached her. Oh my, how grief-stricken she looked standing by herself on the train platform with her suitcase and big tears rolling down her face. Clearly she had no idea what to do next, where to go, who to speak to. So she had not been able to help herself when she heard the terrible news. And what did that mean except that if she was drawn to me in my death she truly loved me in my life. She was so small and ordinary in appearance, how wonderful that I was the only person to know that under her clothes and inside her little rib cage the heart of a great lover was pumping away.

\*

Well there was a bad moment or two. I had to help her sit down. I am here, Winifred, it's all right, I told her over and over again and I held my arms around her shaking, sobbing wracked body.

I wanted us to follow Mama to California, you see. I thought, given all the indications, Winifred would accept herself as an accessory after the fact.

# BABY WILSON

I had taken up with her knowing she was this crazy
lovesick girl. It was against my better judgment. I was
too accustomed to having my life made easy. I was stuck in
my tracks by the smitten sweet smile and the pale eyes.
With straight brown hair she never fussed with but to wash
it. And she wore long cotton dresses and no shoes in the
business district. Karen. A whole year ago. And now she
had gone and done this thing.

She held it out to me all rolled up in a blanket.

Where'd you get that?

Lester, this is our baby. He is named Jesu because he is
a Spanish-looking child. He will be a dark saturnine young
man with slim hips like yours.

The face was still red with its effort to be born, and the
hair was slick with something like pomade, and it had
small dark eyes struggling to see. Around his wrist was a
plastic band.

I don't want to hold him, I said. Take him back.

Oh silly man, she said, smiling, cradling it in her arms. It's not hard to hold a dear child.

No, Karen, I mean take him back to the hospital where you stole him.

I couldn't do that, Lester. I couldn't do that – this is my newborn child, this is my tiny little thing his momma loves so that I am giving to you to be your son.

And she smiled at me that dreamland smile of hers.

She moved her shoulders from side to side and sang to it, but the little arms sort of jerked and waved a bit and she didn't seem to notice. There was a dried blob of blood on the front of its wrappings.

I looked at the clock. It was just noon. Was this a reasonable day, Karen should have been at Nature's Basket doing up her flowers.

I went into the bedroom and put on my jeans and a fresh shirt. I wet my hair and combed it and got a beer from the kitchen.

There were two hospitals in Crenshaw, the private one in the historic district and the county one out by the interstate. What did it matter where she took it from, either one would be just as good. Or I could drive it direct to the police station, not the smartest move in the world. Or I could just take the Durango and leave.

Instead of any of these things, by which I would finally reform into a person who makes executive decisions, I thought to myself I would not want to shock such a woman in her dangerous blissful state of mind, and so went back and tried again, as if you could argue sense into someone who was never too steady to begin with and was now totally bereft of her remaining faculties.

This is wrong, Karen. It is wrong to go around stealing babies.

But this is my baby, she said, staring into its face. I mean our baby, Lester. Yours and mine. I bore it as you conceived it.

I went over to the couch where she had sat down and I looked again at the wristband. It said "Baby Wilson."

My name is not Wilson and your name is not Wilson, I said.

That is a simple clerical error. Jesu is our love child, Lester. He is the indissoluble bond God has placed upon our union. God commanded this. We can never part now – we are a family.

And she looked at me with her pale eyes all adazzle.

Jesu, if it was him, was crying in little yelps and its head was turning this way and that with its mouth open and its little hands were all a-tremor.

I had known she would finally put me at risk. I tried to pay no attention when she stole things and presented them to me, because they were little things and of no use. A Mexican embroidered nightshirt, whereas I like to sleep in the altogether, or a silver money clip in the shape of an L for Lester, like I was some downtown lawyer, or an antique music box, for Christ's sake, that plays "Columbia the Gem of the Ocean," as if anyone would want to hear it more than once. Totally the wrong things for me, if it was me she was stealing for, whereas

I was hard pressed to get a decent meal in this household.

Karen opened her blouse and put the baby to her breast. It hadn't changed any that I could see – of course there was no milk there.

I sat down next to her and pointed the remote at the TV: cartoon, a rerun, puppets, a rerun, nature, a preacher, and then I found the local news station.

Just like them, they hadn't heard the news yet.


Karen, I said, I'll be right back, and I drove into town to the Bluebird. It was lunchtime, busy as hell, and Brenda wasn't too pleased, but seeing the look in my eyes she took a cigarette break out the back door. I told her what was what.

She stood listening, Brenda, and shook her head.

Lester, she said, your brains are in your balls. That is the way you are and the way you'll always be.

Goddamnit, Brenda, it's not something I've done, you understand. Is this what I need to hear from you right now?

She was squinting at me from the smoke drifting up into her eyes.

I said, And you sometimes haven't minded if that's where my brain is, as I recall.

Brenda is as unlike Karen as two women can be. Sturdier in mind, and shaped as if for the Bluebird clientele in her powder blue uniform with the *Brenda* stitched on the bosom pocket.

Are you aware, she said, that kidnapping is a federal offense? Are you aware that if something happens to that infant the both of you – I'm saying the both of you, don't shake your head no – let's see, how do they do it in this state, I forget, electricity or the needle? I mean all Alice in Wonderland will end up is in the loony bin, but you as aiding and abetting – good-bye, Charlie.

I was beginning to feel sick to the stomach standing there out in the sun with the Bluebird garbage bins in full reek.

She ground out her cigarette and took me by the arm and walked me around to the parking lot.

Now, Lester, the first thing is to go to the Kmart and buy you some infant formula, I believe it comes in their own plastic bottles these days. You follow the instructions and feed that baby so it doesn't die, as it surely will if you don't step in here. And while you're at it, buy you an armload of diapers – they come with Velcro now – and a nightie or three and a cap for its head – she looked up at the sky – it's supposed to get cooler later on – and whatever else you see there in Infants and Toddlers that might come in useful. You understand me?

I nodded.

And then when it turns out you haven't killed that child, you get it back to its rightful parents as soon as you possibly can, anyway you can, and see to it that your darling poetess up there on Cloud Nine takes the rap that is justly hers to take. Do you hear me?

I nodded.

43

Brenda opened the door for me and saw me up behind the wheel.

And, Lester? If I don't hear on the TV tonight that you've settled this to a happy conclusion, I personally will call the cops. You understand me?

Thanks, Brenda.

She slammed the door. And don't ever try to see me anymore, Lester, you asshole, she said.


I had done everything Brenda said to do by way of food and sanitation, and now there was peace in the house. I didn't want to alarm Karen in any way, so I treated her with nothing but cooperation. By the time I had gotten back from the store, she had just begun to realize a baby needed taking care of. She was so grateful she hugged me, and I helped her fuss over that child as if it was truly ours. Isn't he the sweetest thing? Karen said. How he seems to know us – oh that is so dear! Look at that sweet face. He is surely the most beautiful baby I ever have seen!

Now, with everything calmed down and both Karen and Baby Wilson asleep on our bed, it was time to do some thinking. I put on the five o'clock news to get the lay of the land.

Oh my. The Crenshaw Commissioner of Police saying the entire CPD had been put on alert and deployed throughout the city to find the infant and apprehend the kidnapper or kidnappers. He'd also notified the FBI.

Hey, I said, it is just my slightly crazy girl Karen. You

don't have to worry, we're not kidnappers, man.

The female they wanted for questioning was probably in her twenties, young, white, about five-six, slight of build with straight brown hair. She had brought a bouquet of flowers and, when approached by a nurse, claimed to be a friend of Mrs. Wilson.

She was that cool, my Karen?

Behind the commissioner was a worried-looking hospital official and, I supposed, the nurse in question, tearful now for having turned her back for a moment to look for a vase.

Then a doctor stepped to the microphone and said whoever had the baby to remember that there was an open wound at the site of the umbilical cord. It should be kept clean and dressed with an antibacterial agent and a fresh bandage at least once a day.

Well, I knew that. I had seen it for myself. I'd found the Polysporin in the medicine chest I had once bought for a cut on my forehead and applied it only after I washed my hands. I am not stupid. The doctor said the baby should only have sponge baths until the wound healed. I would have figured that out, too.

A reporter asked if a ransom note had been received. That really got me riled. Of course not, you moron, I said. What do you think we are? No ransom note as yet, the commissioner said, emphasizing the "as yet," which offended me even more.

Then we were back in the studio with the handsome news anchor: He said Mrs. Wilson the mother was under sedation. He quoted Mr. Wilson the father as saying he didn't understand – they were not rich people, that he was a CPA who worked for his living like everyone else.

I had seen enough. I woke up Karen and hustled her and the baby and all the Kmart paraphernalia into the Durango. Why, whatever is the matter, Lester? Karen said. She was still half asleep. Are we going somewhere? She looked frightened for a moment until I put Baby Wilson in her arms. I ran back to the house and grabbed some clothes and things for each of us. Then I ran back again and turned off the lights and locked the door.

I could imagine them any minute coming up the road and through the woods around us at the same time. We were in a cul-de-sac at the end of a dirt road here. I drove down to the two-lane. It was a mile from there to the freeway ramp. I pointed east for Nevada, though not planning to go there necessarily but just to be out on the highway away from town, feeling safer on the move, though expecting any minute to see a cop car in the rearview.

I wasn't worried about Brenda – she would think twice before getting involved. But I reasoned that if the police were smart they would talk to every florist in the city. Of course their being Crenshaw's finest, it was only even odds they would make the connection to an employee of Nature's Basket who had not shown up for work, one Karen Robileaux, age twenty-six. But even odds was not good enough as far as I was concerned, besides which the FBI were getting on the case, so say the odds were now sixty-forty, and if they made an I.D. of Karen it would be too late for an anonymous return of the baby. And if they came knocking on the door before I had the chance to deliver him back of our own accord, as appeared likely, there would be no alleviating circumstances for a judge to consider, that I could see.

And so we were out of there.


I had picked up her shoulder bag when running out of the house. Of course it was of Indian design, knitted, with all sorts of jagged lines, sectioned like a map in different colors of sand and rust and aqua. Inside, she kept not what women usually keep in their bags, no lipstick or powder compacts or portable tampon containers or any such normal things as that. She had some crumbs of dried flowers and a packet of Kleenex and her housekeys and a paperback book about the Intergalactic Council, a kind of UN of advanced civilizations around the universe and how it was trying to send messages of peace to Earth. It was a non-fiction book, she had told me all about it. She had been thinking of becoming an Earth Representative of the Council. And two crumpled dollar bills and a handful of change.

Karen, don't you have any money? Didn't you get paid this week?

Oh I forgot. Yes, Lester, let's see, she said and rooted about in the pocket of her dress. And she handed me her pay envelope.

She had her hundred and twenty in there. I was carrying

thirty-five in my wallet. Not great. I could cover gas, food, and a motel room for a night.

After a couple of hours on the road I was calming down. It occurred to me, despite everything I was not mad at Karen. Given her state of mind she couldn't be held responsible. If anyone, I was the one to blame for not springing into action the minute she walked in the door with the kid. And she was so trusting, sitting up there beside me with Baby Wilson in her arms and her eyes on the road ahead. She didn't ask where we were going, not that I could have told her. And the moving car seemed to soothe him, too. He was quiet in her arms. A weird feeling, something like a pride of ownership, came over me, that I would compare now to falling asleep at the wheel. Migod, I woke up quickly enough.

By now it had gotten dark, it was all desert now, the road flat and straight. Karen opened her window and leaned out to see the stars. I had to slow down so Baby Wilson would not have a cold wind blowing into his face. I stuck my hand over the back of the seat and rummaged around till I found the package of diapers. I pulled one out and told her to put it around his little head.

Babies don't get sick the first three months of their life, Karen said. No viruses or anything. They are automatically insured by God for three months exactly, did you know that, Lester?

But she did as I asked.

By midnight I had us tucked away in a Days Inn outside of Dopple City, Nevada. So without consciously thinking about it till we were practically there, this is where I had meant to come.

I brought in a hamburger dinner, french fries, chicken wings, a milkshake, and for Karen a garden salad. She never drank anything but water. I left her sitting on one of the double beds and feeding the child. I went outside for a smoke and then got back in the SUV.

I knew Dopple. It was a city in its dreams only – what, a railroad yard, a string of car dealerships? It wasn't much of anything. Anyone could find the strip by seeing where the night sky was lit up.

I decided on Fortunato's. The lady dealers, with their little black bow ties and white shirts and black vests and ass-tight slacks, were the one bit of class. Bells ringing, someone singing with a karaoke, the usual din of losers. A cheap mob place trying to be Vegas with an understocked bar and slots from yesteryear. It smelled, too, like there was a stable or a cow barn out back.

In the men's room, where the floor was all wet and some drunk had lost it, I carefully combed my hair. Then I went out and sat down at a five-dollar table that looked about right and bought fifty dollars in chips. Little blond lady dealer, a pit man just behind her. Four decks in the shoe, but my system is not counting cards. My system is betting modestly while sitting next to a high roller with a big stack in front of him. Kind who talks too much and swivels around with each winning hand to see if he's gathered the audience he deserves.

I didn't look at the dealer, but smiled as if to myself

49

every now and then. I was very quiet. When I doubled, if
the pit man had moved on, I put down a chip for her. She
didn't look at me, but nodded slightly and smiled as if to
herself. Tiny mouth but well shaped. There arose a sym-
pathy between us. It's not as if any cheating goes on, it's
more like a flirtation through the cards. Things happen. At
the end of a half hour it was as if she'd taken the edge of
her plump little hand and cut one of the high roller's stacks
and slid it over to me. I got up at that point – it was supposed to be a fun thing, nothing to take too far. That would
lack class, ruin the whole game between us. I left twenty for
her and cashed in for a hundred twenty-five dollars net.

It was a short drive to the Mexican part of town. Dark
there, quiet, not many lights. I parked into the curb, rolled
down the window, and sat there and had a smoke, and
pretty soon a kid came along. He couldn't have been more
than thirteen, fourteen. Peered in at me for a good look.
When I told him what I was buying, he went to the front of
my car and looked at the California plate. Then he went
around a corner and a few minutes later someone who
could have been his mother was standing at my window.
She was a heavyset woman with a handsome broad face
and a black dress too tight for her, but she acted tired, or
fed up. She wanted one-fifty for a sixpack, which was
cheap enough, but I told her as honestly as I could I only
had one and a quarter to spend. She said something indi-
cating her disgust in Spanish, but then she nodded and I
drove away with two Visas, two MasterCards, and two
Amexes, one of them Gold.

What was I up to if not executive decisions? I felt almost proud of myself by the time I got back to the motel. Karen was asleep with her arm around the infant. Her shift had ridden up. She was weird and maybe even a witch of a sort, but those were the smoothest young legs and artfully draped crescents of backside a man could ever hope to gaze upon. But I was tired too and decided to wait till morning. I conformed one of my driver's licenses, practiced my signature, and then went to sleep in the other bed thinking what a great country this was.

Of course the infernal problem remained, whatever the stupid mood I happened to be in. How was I going to get little junior away from Karen without making her crazier than she was? And if I managed that, how to avoid the law while finding a way to deliver him to his proper parents? And thirdly, how to keep Karen out of a U.S. District Court, as well as the newspapers as an object of public odium, to say nothing of myself?

And then in the morning of course she was so busy with the baby that she didn't have time for me. Or inclination. Everything was Jesu this and Jesu that, all her love flowing out of her and none of it coming in my direction. She sent me off for more supplies, so careless of my feelings she didn't even feel it necessary to explain that the baby was taking all her weakened strength, as if she was a real mother recovering from the act of giving birth. She just expected me to understand that from the way she moved about, holding her hand in the small of her back for a moment of thought, or blowing back from the corner of her mouth a strand of hair that had fallen over her eye because both her hands were busy diapering the kid, and so on.

It is strange how different the same woman can be at different times, even a lovesick crazy one like this, who was so moony about me from the first moment I caught her attention when I walked into Nature's Basket to wire flowers for my mother's birthday in Illinois. There was this lovely girl in a long dress and barefooted who seemed to have risen out of the smell of earth and the heavy humidity you get in a florist. Karen looked at me as if struck dumb. She tucked her hair behind her ears and said it was nice that I had a mother I thought so well of. I didn't tell her otherwise. I went along with her illusion, whereas the twenty-five dollars I laid down for the mixed bouquet was an investment against a return of ten times or twenty times that which I hoped to wheedle out of the old bat after a decent interval.

So after I get back with doughnuts and coffee, and a yogurt for Karen, and this and that from the drugstore, it starts to rain in Dopple City. Lightning and thunder, an unlikely spring torrent, and what does she do but take Baby Wilson outside behind the Days Inn, where she steps over the scraggly attempt at landscaping and walks out into the desert dirt, laughing and hugging the poor child and holding her head up to drink rainwater while not listening to what I am saying, and shaking me off when I try to hustle her back inside. And as suddenly as it came the rain passes, and Karen is standing there with her hair wet as if she's just had a shower and she says, Look, my sweet baby, you see what God is doing? And to me she says, You too, Lester. Wait for the runoff, where the rivulets leave their traces, keep your eyes focused – it is the pure magic of the desert you are about to see.

And all she meant was those desert wildflowers that hurry to blossom from the least encouragement of rain, which they did – little settlements of blue and yellow and white spikes and petals and tiny cups in the declivities, clustered close to the land as if not wanting to take the chance of growing up too far away from it, flowers that you don't actually see opening but just have the feeling that they were there all along only you didn't happen to notice them before.

And that was pretty if you go for that sort of thing, but the child still couldn't see, although he seemed to be peering out from under her hand, which she held over his head like an umbrella, and for a moment I had the ridiculous feeling of real communication between them, this mad girl and a stolen infant just two or three days old who were now poking about together under the sun out there in the flowering desert behind the Days Inn.

I left them there and got the keys to the Durango and took it down the highway to a used-car place. I wanted to get out of Dopple City as soon as possible. My theory was to keep moving if nothing else. Besides which I did not want to have to pay another day's rent on the motel room, the checkout time for which was twelve noon.

The Durango was registered in both our names, although in truth it was Karen's savings that had bought it, but under my influence, I might add, since I had always held Durangos in high esteem.

It was already used when we bought it, though in reasonable condition, with just fifty thousand miles on the odometer, which I had since added twenty to, but the front tires were almost new, which is what I explained to the guy at the car lot, uselessly, since he would only give me seven-fifty for it, six if I wanted cash. I took the six hundred. He was a short, fat underhanded thief in a white shirt and string tie but then again did not ask too many questions as he unscrewed my plates and handed them to me.

His man gave me a ride a mile down the road to the Southwest Car Rental and I used my Amex Gold to secure a Windstar van, whose greatest if not only attribute was a Nevada license plate.

It was in this sad, shining new van that I wouldn't ordinarily be caught dead in that I packed up my imitation wife and child and headed west back to California. I had no idea what to do. But we were well disguised in our domestic vehicle and a little baby boy adorably asleep in the new car chair I had gotten him. Karen stroked the upholstery. She marveled at the drink containers at each seat. She accepted the Windstar without question as she did any mysterious moves on my part. My feeling about things began to change: I had cash in my pocket and now some pride in my heart, because Karen loved the new car. She turned the radio on, and there we were, heading west with the sun behind us and the great Patsy Cline singing "Sweet Dreams of You," Karen giving me a sly amused and weirdly sane glance that caused me nearly to swerve into the opposite lane as we sang along with Patsy, *I know I should hate you the whole night through, instead of having sweet dreams of you.*

Now I do admit that there came over me an idea I not only hadn't considered but that wouldn't have come even glancingly to my mind before this moment, which was to go with the flow – to take my girl's madness for my own, to embrace it as, before all this happened, I had customarily embraced her. Why not? Baby Wilson already had a certain character that I found agreeable. He cried only when he had to, and seemed thoughtful most of the time, if that was possible, full of serious attention to the new world in which he found himself, as if, seeing it only as a blur, he was making up for it by listening very carefully. And though Karen told me that what I thought was a smile as he looked at me was in reality of bit of indigestion, it was hard for me not to smile back. Karen seemed to have acquired the wise love that mothers have the instant they become mothers, as if the hormones or whatever maternal chemicals were involved had begun to operate within her from the moment she calmly walked out of that hospital with some other woman's newborn in her arms.

I didn't know anything about the Wilsons except that Mr. Wilson was an accountant, which didn't foretell a particularly exciting life for this kid, who had already seen, and not yet a week old, two states and a rare rain in the desert that not many people not living in the desert would ever see. And his beautiful though self-appointed and by law criminally insane mother had picked one tiny blue flower and put its stem in his little hand, and his fingers had curled around it, automatically of course, but he still clutched it, though fast asleep in his car chair as we crossed the state line into California.

And from all of this and the sun lighting our way ahead like a golden road, I had this revelation of a new life for myself, a life I had never thought of aspiring to, where I would be someone's husband and someone else's father, dependable, holding down a full-time job, and building a place in the world for himself and his family. So that when he died they would mourn grievously and bless his departing spirit for the love and respectable life he had given them.

A special news bulletin on the radio was like cold water on my face: Baby Wilson's parents had received a ransom note.

We were about a hundred miles east of Crenshaw. I pulled over to the side of the road.

The details of the note had not been divulged, but it was believed the Wilsons intended to meet the kidnapper's demands.

Goddamn!

What, Lester?

Can you believe this?

I pounded the steering wheel. The baby woke and began to cry. Karen reached back and unbuckled him and lifted him over the seat and held him in her arms as if to protect him from me.

Lester, you're frightening us!

Can you believe the evil in this world? That some slime would con those poor people and cash in on their suffering?

She was silent for a moment. She said, I do believe there is evil in this world, yes, but I believe people can be redeemed? Her voice clouded up. She could barely finish the sentence. She began rocking the kid in her arms and soon the tears were coming and now I had the two of them bawling away.

I got out of the van and lit a cigarette and paced up and down the grass shoulder. A car sped by and its wind made the van shudder. Then another. I wanted to be in one of those cars. There was some sort of green crop growing in bunches low to the ground behind the fence and it seemed to go on for miles. I wanted to be the farmer out here in the middle of nowhere quietly growing his cash crop of whatever it was – spinach or cauliflower or some other inedible damn vegetable. I wanted to be anyone but who I was and anywhere but where I was. What was I supposed to do now?

I motioned for her to roll down her window: Has it occurred to you, Karen, that you have provided him or them the opportunity?

Gone were all my diplomatic strategies. All the anger that I had pent up cascaded over this sad pathetic girl sitting rocking the baby in her arms, and her pale eyes reddened and enlarged with the tears rolling down her cheeks.

Yes, you have stirred up something really grand, you know that? You have inspired others to do evil, Karen Robileaux. And not only this slime or slimes. Supposing he really had possession of the baby? Is it in the baby's interest of safety to have the news broadcast all around the country that there is a ransom note? Of course not. How could this slimeball trust them now, these poor parents, thinking they had told everyone about his private communication. What would you do under the circumstances if you couldn't trust the parents to deal without calling in the cops, the FBI, and the media – I mean this is a goddamn radio station in Los Angeles. Los Angeles! They don't give a shit if the baby turns up dead. They just want people to listen so they can sell their advertising. They are happy to violate such delicate confidences. They are proud to be good reporters! So the evil is going out in all directions, Karen, like radio waves from an antenna!

He can't do anything bad to this baby, she sobbed. None of them can. He doesn't have this baby. I have this baby, she said, kissing the child fervently on the cheeks, on his head, every part of him that was not swaddled.

Well maybe not, I said, quieter now. But how do the Wilsons know that? He has already done something to them when they find out he is a fraud and a hoax and they are who knows how many thousands of dollars poorer. And not only that, I said more to myself than to her, everyone thinks now you have an accomplice, a male accomplice, because no woman alone who stole a child would do it for purposes of ransom.

Karen opened the door and stepped out of the van and handed me Baby Wilson, and then went off a ways on the shoulder behind a tree and lifted her dress and squatted down to pee.

I had not held him before to any extent. He was a warm little fellow. I could feel his heart beat, and he squirmed around a bit trying to look at me who was holding him. And he had stopped crying.

When Karen came back she took Baby Wilson and got in the van and sat there frowning and staring straight ahead and she wasn't crying anymore, either. It was like she was waiting for the car to move, as if it really didn't need a driver to get up there beside her and put the key in the ignition.

A few miles on at the edge of a town I pulled into a gas station with a convenience store. I bought us bottled water and presented one to Karen by way of a peace offering.

59

Without looking at me she took it. I bought the newspapers they carried, the local and the L.A. and San Diego papers. They all had the story, they were blissed-out with excitement. And every story came with a composite police drawing of someone who looked like Karen though with her ears grown bigger and her mouth thinner and her eyes transplanted from someone else. It was both not a good likeness and too close for comfort.

I tossed the papers away. I didn't feel the need to show her anything more by way of persuasion. She had no voice in the matter as far as I was concerned. We drove on and this turned out to be a well-groomed little town, with big trees shading the streets and the retail stores uniformly in good taste so as not to offend the eye. And there was nobody in sight, as if the townsfolk were having their afternoon nap, even the police.

It hit me then, my idea: If the story was in every paper, if it was all over the damn state, did it matter where we dropped off Baby Wilson? And I thought, Why not here? And if not now, when?

I peered right and left as I rolled to stop at each corner until I saw something along the lines of what I wanted – a neat white stucco church with a red barrel-tile roof. It was a Catholic church, as uniformly tasteful as everything else in this town. It had a Christ on the cross in relief on the stucco steeple. I can't now remember the Saintly name of it, even the town's name escapes me – this was a moment of such stressful fatedness that the surroundings remain in my mind only as bodily impressions. I remember the sun on my neck as I carried the car seat by its handles as a portable carryall for the baby after Karen had been in there a few minutes, I remember my instructions to her beforehand as we sat in the van with the motor running in the neatly ruled empty parking lot around the side, and though the air-conditioning was on I felt the sweat dripping down the small of my back.

It was very peculiar that she seemed as ready as I was, as if somewhere, at some moment – I couldn't have told you when – we had made magnetic contact. As if it had never been otherwise than that we were both sane and synchronized in our thought. So I experienced something also like a feeling of estrangement as I realized, looking at her, that I loved Karen Robileaux. I loved her. I mean it just came over me – an incredible welcoming rush of gladness that welled up in my throat and threatened to spill out of my eyes. I loved her. Her frail being was strong. Her kookiness was mystical. And it was even eerier to hear in my mind, at last, what she had been telling me time and time again before this all happened – how she adored me, how she actually did love me in all the ways that people understand as love. It was a bonding that was true if it was this scary. Of course I said nothing, and did not declare myself. I really didn't have to. She knew. Our intimacy was in the fact of our conspiring together as she concentrated on what I was saying with her pale wolf eyes staring into mine, so much so that, once she got out of the car and walked up the steps into the church, I wondered if this hadn't really been her plan and that she had brought me to this moment as I believed I had brought her. Because I remember her only problem was technical, whereas you might have expected much more in the way of resistance.

Lester, she said, I don't know the right words for confessing.

It's okay, I said. Just go in there and sit down in that box they have. It is somewhere off to the side. You don't have to be Catholic for them to listen to you. When he hears you, the priest will sit down on the other side of the screen, and you just tell him you want to confess something. And he will listen and never betray your trust that it is just between the two of you. And you don't have to cross yourself or anything – he will tell you what to do if you put it in the form of asking for his advice. I mean you know what he will say. And you will thank him, and you will mean it, and maybe thank God too that there are people who are sworn to do this for a living.

And what will he do then?

See, I have to believe priests read the papers and watch the TV like everyone else, so he will know what baby you are talking about. He will say, And where is the Wilson baby now? And you will tell him, Father, the baby is here. You will find him in his carryall just inside the front door. And a paper sack with his formula and his diapers and a tube of Polysporin for his bellybutton.

And when he gets up and runs down the aisle, you slip out the side door to right here where we are parked.

Karen is a brave woman. She has always been brave, and never more than in this moment. She walked in there with her skirt swaying from her lovely hips and her hair, which she had tied up in a ponytail given the solemnity of the occasion, also swinging from side to side, and for the same reason her usually bare feet in a pair of sandals.

But before she took her deep breath and stepped down from the Windstar, she held the baby in her arms and caressed his round little head and brushed his dark hairs with the tips of her fingers as he stared up at her in his impassive manner and then looked away. And then Karen slipped him gently into my arms like a friend of the mother's who has been given the privilege for just that moment of holding another woman's child.

That whole day as we drove she slept in the backseat, curled up with her hands under her chin. I had decided to head north, staying off the freeways for the most part. When it was evening, I pulled into a motel and she went right from the car to the bed, where she got under the covers and went immediately back to sleep. I didn't take any chance that she would wake up and watch the TV so I pulled the plug and bent it out of shape before I went to the restaurant they had there and watched for myself on the bar TV. Mr. and Mrs. Wilson were shown hugging their baby and laughing through their tears. They were not the youngest of couples, they were both on the portly side, and in fact Mr. Wilson had a paunch on him to make me think I would never let myself go that way. And it turned out they had six other children of various sizes standing

around the couch looking at the camera with what I recognized as the same unsmiling quietness of expression as
Baby Wilson himself.

Meanwhile an announcer was telling the story of the
return, and quoting Mr. Wilson saying he and his wife
were so happy they forgave whoever had kidnapped their
child, but before I could breathe a sigh of relief, the
camera cut to the FBI official in charge of the investigation
and he said that the FBI would continue the search – that,
regardless of the outcome, a federal crime had been committed and it was never up to the Wilsons to decide
whether or not to prosecute. And then another shot of the
bad drawing of Karen.

In the gift shop there I bought a pair of sunglasses and
an Angels baseball cap, and we got up at dawn and drove
away. Karen wore the glasses and that cap with her hair
tucked up inside all the way through California. I used the
credit cards sparingly, each one never more than once until
the last one, which I hazarded a couple of times and then
threw it away, not wanting to press my luck, and now we
were down to our diminishing cash funds.

In San Francisco, I parked Karen in a movie theater
and went around to Noe Street to see if Fran still lived
there. She did. When she opened her door, she said, Well,
will you look what the cat dragged in! Fran was never the
sort to bear a grudge. She was a song stylist who made her
living singing in clubs. She had a housemate now, a kind of
blowsy older woman, who nevertheless had the tact to
excuse herself on some errand or other, probably to her

chosen bar. I visited with Frannie almost the whole two hours of a feature movie, and then she walked with me to the ATM at the local grocery. As I left, I swore I would return her generosity in full. I knew she didn't believe me, because she gave a good-hearted laugh and said time would tell and she was smiling and shaking her head as I waved and turned the corner.

Just before the Oregon state line, I removed the Nevada plates from the Windstar and replaced them with the Durango's old California plates.

In Seattle, we took the ferry to Canada, standing at the rail in the gray and green mist of that day, with the foghorns coming over the water and the smell of the sea and gulls appearing and disappearing in the bad visibility. Karen loved this part of the trip. There was a new peace between us, and she held my arm with both her hands with a kind of fervent wifeliness.

At the hotel in Vancouver we resumed our lovemaking as in our first days together and it was action-packed. She had really come awake to life as I realized now, reflecting on the last months between us, when she was more with-drawn than I wanted to admit.

Vancouver is a squeaky-clean town, like all of Canada that I have ever seen – glass office buildings the color of the sky, the waterside filled with flag-flying yachts and motorboats, the downtown without litter of any kind, and everyone going about their business so as not to disturb anyone else. Not a town you want to stay in very long. But you find thir. gs if you look and I found a man in the import-export business who would take the Windstar off my hands, and if he gave me three thousand American for it, I knew he would clear at least ten at the other end.

Then I bought Karen an opal engagement ring and a gold wedding band for one thousand Canadian, though we didn't actually get legally married till we were settled in this town in Alaska, where she is known not as Karen Robileaux but as Mrs. Lester Romanowski, although she doesn't get around enough to be known very well in her condition but stays up there in this hillside cabin we rent and tends her garden and cooks good things, not only for me but for herself, since she is eating for two, while in the meantime I am working down below, at sea level, between the mountains and the waterside, which is where the town is crammed.

I have different jobs, one scrubbing pots and pans in this phony frontier restaurant, where the monster hamburger menu is up on blackboards and the bartender has a red beard and wears a lumberjack shirt with the sleeves rolled and there is sawdust on the floor. I also drive a school bus in the early morning and mid-afternoon, and another job, when I have to, is the slime line, which is where they handle the fish off the boats – a heavy-hauling, slippery job requiring rubber apron and gloves and hip boots and a shower and a good deodorant at the end of the shift.

Just now I have a new opportunity on the weekend. I put on a funny bear costume and meet the cruise-ship pas-sengers as they come down the gangway. I do it because, A, nobody knows it's me in that stupid outfit and, B, it gives me a chance to get close to those ships without drawing attention to myself. I dance the ladies around a bit and make them laugh and pose with them for a photo to record their historic visit to Alaska.

On my off day, Karen and I have found a place to watch the bears fishing in the shallows for their salmon dinner. Lots of birds busy in the forest, and animals I don't get up out of bed to identify rustle around the cabin at night. Up through the tops of the trees every morning we see the black bald eagle that lives up the side of the mountain and likes to soar about in the thermals.

Most people living here don't quite fit into the greater U.S. for one reason or another, so nobody asks too many questions. Everyone I've met mostly has an attitude of big plans for themselves, which I certainly can appreciate. I'm beginning to think my big plan must have something to do with those cruise ships. They sail up every day to rest their block-long hulls against the dockside. When the tourists pour down the gangways to flow through the streets, well, this, plus the fish, is what keeps the Panhandle in the money. But more of the money stays aboard at the gaming tables and so I'm thinking I might find a way to I.D. as a passenger, take an overnight cruise to the next landing, come back flush the next day – I don't know – the modus is there, it is only a matter of time till it makes itself known to me.

Karen hugs me when I come home and always has a good dinner waiting, and sits across the table with her chin in her hand and stares at me as I eat. Of course she praises the reformed man I have become, and as a person who has not been without bold ideas of her own, she can appreciate that I am alert and ready for inspiration. But basically she has no mind for anything but the baby growing inside her. She has a wise, contented smile these days, my young wife. No one meeting her for the first time would think she was anything but sane. She said last night that she hopes I don't mind not being consulted but she got used to the name Jesu and so that is what he will be called.

# JOLENE: A LIFE

S he married Mickey Holler when she was fifteen. Married him to get out of her latest foster home where her so-called dad used to fool with her, get her to hold him, things like that. Even before her menses started. And her foster mom liked to slap her up the head for no reason. Or for every reason. So she married Mickey. And he loved her – that was a plus. She had never had that experience before. It made her look at herself in the mirror and do things with her hair. He was twenty, Mickey. Real name Mervin. He was a sweet boy if without very much upstairs, as she knew even from their first date. He had a heel that didn't touch the ground and weak eyes but he was not the kind to lay a hand on a woman. And she could tell him what she wanted, like a movie, or a grilled-cheese sandwich and a chocolate shake, and it became his purpose in life. He loved her, he really did, even if he didn't know much about it.

But anyway she was out of the house now, and wearing a wedding ring to South Sumter High. Some of the boys said smutty things but the girls looked upon her with a new respect.

Mickey's Uncle Phil had come to the justice of the peace with them to be best man. After the ceremony he grinned and said Welcome to our family, Jolene honey, and gave her a big hug that lasted a mite too long. Uncle Phil was like a father to Mickey and employed him to drive one of the trucks in his home oil delivery business. Mickey Holler was almost an orphan. His real father was in the state penitentiary with no parole for the same reason his mother was in the burial ground behind the First Baptist Church. Jolene asked Mickey, as she thought permissible now that she was a relation, what his mother had done to deserve her fate. But he got all flustered when he tried to talk about it. It happened when he was only twelve. She was left to gather for herself that his father was a crazy drunk who had done bad things even before this happened. But anyway that was why Jolene was living now with Mickey under the same roof with his Uncle Phil and Aunt Kay.

Aunt Kay was real smart. She was an assistant manager in the Southern People's Bank across the square from the courthouse. So between her and Uncle Phil's oil business, they had a nice ranch house with a garden out back and a picnic table and two hammocks between the trees.

Jolene liked the room she and Mickey occupied, though it looked into the driveway, and she had what she could do to keep it nice, with Mickey dropping his greasy coveralls on the floor. But she understood the double obligations of being a wife and an unpaying boarder besides. As she was home from school before anyone finished their jobs for the day, she tried to make herself useful. She would have an hour or so to do some of her homework and then she would go into the kitchen and put up something for everyone's dinner.

Jolene had always liked school – she felt at home there. Her favorite subject was art. She had been drawing from the time she was in third grade, when the class had done a mural of the Battle of Gettysburg and she drew more of it than anyone. She couldn't do much art now at this time in her life as a married woman, not being just for herself anymore. But she still noticed things. She was someone who had an eye for what wants to be drawn. Mickey had a white hairless chest with a collarbone that stood out across from shoulder to shoulder like he was someone's beast of burden. And a long neck and a backbone that she could use to do sums. He surely did love her – he cried sometimes he loved her so much – but that was all. She had a sixteenth birthday and he bought her a negligee he picked out himself at Berman's department store. It was three sizes too big. Jolene could take it back for exchange, of course, but she had the unsettling thought that as Mickey's wife all that would happen in her life to come was she would grow into something that size. He liked to watch her doing her homework, which made her realize he had no ambition, Mickey Holler. He would never run a business and play golf on the weekend like Uncle Phil. He was a day-to-day person. He did not ever talk about

73

buying his own home, or moving toward anything that would make things different for them than they were now. She could think this of him even though she liked to kiss his pale chest and run her fingers over the humps of his backbone.

Uncle Phil was tall with a good strong jaw and a head of shining black hair he combed in a kind of wave, and he had a deep voice and he joked around with a lot of self-assurance, and dark meaningful eyes – oh, he was a man, of that there was no doubt. At first it made Jolene nervous when he would eye her up and down. Or he would sing a line from a famous love song to her. *You are so beautiful to mee!* And then he would laugh to let her know it was all just the same horsing around as he was accustomed to doing. He was tanned from being out on the county golf course, and even the slight belly he had on him under his knit shirt seemed just right. The main thing about him was that he enjoyed his life, and he was popular – they had their social set, though you could see most of their friends came through him.

Aunt Kay was not exactly the opposite of Phil, but she was one who attended to business. She was a proper sort who never sat back with her shoes off, and though kind and correct as far as Jolene was concerned, clearly would have preferred to have her home to herself now that Mickey had someone to take care of him. Jolene knew this – she didn't have to be told. She could work her fingers to the bone and Aunt Kay would still never love her. Aunt Kay was a Yankee and had come to live in the South because of a job offer. She and Uncle Phil had been married fifteen years. She called him Phillip, which Jolene thought was putting on airs. She wore suits and panty hose, always, and blouses with collars buttoned to the neck. She was no beauty, but you could see what had interested Phil — her very light blue icy eyes, maybe, and naturally blond hair, and she had the generous figure that required a panty girdle, which she was never without.

But now Uncle Phil got in the habit of waking them up in the morning, coming into their room without knocking and saying in his deep voice, "Time for work, Mickey Holler!" but looking at Jolene in the meantime as she pulled the covers up to her chin.

She knew the man was doing something he shouldn't be doing with that wake-up routine and it made her angry but she didn't know what she could do about it. Mickey seemed blind to the fact that his own uncle, his late mother's brother, had an eye for her. At the same time she was excited to have been noticed by this man of the world. She knew that as a handsome smiling fellow with white teeth, Phil would be quite aware of his effect on women, so she made a point of seeming to be oblivious of him as anything but her husband's uncle and employer. But this became more and more difficult, living in the same house with him. She found herself thinking about him. In her mind Jolene made up a story: how gradually, over time, it would become apparent that she and Uncle Phil were meant for each other. How an understanding would arise between them and go on for some years until, possibly,

Aunt Kay died, or left him – it wasn't all that clear in Jolene's mind.

But Uncle Phil was not one for dreaming. One afternoon she was scrubbing their kitchen floor for them, down on her knees in her shorts with her rump up in the air, and he had come home early, in that being his own boss he could come and go as he liked. She was humming "I Want to Hold Your Hand" and didn't hear him.

He stood in the door watching how the scrubbing motion was rendered on her behind, and no sooner did she realize she was not alone than he was lifting her from the waist in her same kneeling position and carrying her that way into his bedroom, the scrub brush still in her hand.

That night in her own bed she could still smell Uncle Phil's aftershave lotion and feel the little cotton balls of their chenille bedspread in the grasp of her fingers. She was too sore even for Mickey's fumblings.

And that was the beginning. In all Jolene's young life she had never been to where she couldn't wait to see someone. She tried to contain herself, but her schoolwork began to fall off, though she had always been a conscientious student even if not the smartest brain in her class. But it was that way with Phil, too – it was so intense and constant that he was no longer laughing. It was more like they were equals in their magnetic attraction. They just couldn't get enough. It was every day, always while Aunt Kay was putting up her numbers in the Southern People's Bank and Mickey, poor Mickey was riding his oil route as Uncle Phil devised it to the furthermost reaches of the town line and beyond.

Well, the passion between people can never be anything but drawn to a conclusion by the lawful spouses around them, and after a month or two of this everyone knew it, and the crisis came banging open the bedroom door shouting her name, and all at once Mickey was riding Phil's back like a monkey, beating him about the head and crying all the while, and Phil, in his skivvies, with Mickey pounding him, staggered around the combined living and dining room till he backpedaled the poor boy up against their big TV and smashed him through the screen. Jolene, in her later reflections, when she had nothing in the world to do but pass the time, remembered everything she remembered the bursting sound of the TV glass, she remembered how surprised she was to see how skinny Phil's legs were, and that the sun through the blinds was so bright because daylight saving had come along unbeknownst to the lovers, which was why the working people had got home before they were supposed to. But at the time there was no leisure for thought. Aunt Kay was dragging her by the hair through the hall over the shag carpet and into the kitchen across the fake-tile flooring and she was out the kitchen door, kicked down the back steps, and thrown out like someone's damn cat and yowling like one, too.

Jolene waited out there by the edge of the property, crouching in the bushes in her shift with her arms folded across her breasts. She waited for Phil to come out and take her away, but he never did. Mickey is the one who opened the door. He stood there looking at her, in the quiet outside, while from the house they listened to the shouting and the sound of things breaking. Mickey's hair was sticking up and his glasses were bent broken across his nose. Jolene called to him. She was crying; she wanted him to forgive her and tell her it was all right. But what he did, her Mickey, he got in his pickup in his bloody shirt and drove away. That was what Jolene came to think of as the end of Chapter 1 in her life story, because where Mickey drove to was the middle of the Catawba River Bridge, and there he stopped and with the engine still running he jumped off into that rocky river and killed himself.

More than one neighbor must have seen her wandering the streets, and by and by a police cruiser picked her up, and first she was taken to the emergency room, where it was noted that her vital signs were okay, though they showed her where a clump of her red hair had been pulled out. Then she was put into a motel off the interstate while the system figured out what to do with her. She was a homewrecker but also a widow but also a juvenile with no living relatives. The fosters she had left to marry Mickey would take no responsibility for her. Time passed. She watched soaps. She cried. A matron was keeping an eye on her morning and night. Then a psychiatrist who worked for the county came to interview her. A day after that she was driven to a court hearing with testimony by this county psychiatrist she had told her story to in all honesty, and that was something that embittered her as the double-cross of all time, because on his recommendation she was remanded to the juvenile loony bin until such time as she was to become a reasonable adult able to take care of herself.

Well, so there she was moping about on their pills, half asleep for most of the day and night, and of course as she quickly learned this was no place to regain her sanity, if she ever lost it in the first place, which she knew just by looking at who else was there that she hadn't. About two months into the hell there, they one morning took off her usual gray hanging frock and put her in a recognizable dark dress, though a size too big, and fixed her hair with a barrette and drove her in a van to the courthouse once again, though this time it was for her testimony as to her relations with Uncle Phil, who was there at the defense table looking awful. She didn't know what was different about him till she realized his hair was without luster and, in fact, gray. Then she knew that all this time she had been so impressed he had been dyeing it. He was hunched over from the fix he was in and he never looked at her, this man of the world. A little of the old feeling arose in her and she was angry with herself but she couldn't help it. She waited for some acknowledgment, but it never came. What it was, Aunt Kay had kicked him out, he was sleeping in his office, his business had gone down the tube, and none of his buddies would play golf with him anymore.

Jolene was called upon to show the judge that she was, at sixteen, underage for such doings, which made Phil a statutory rapist. There was a nice legal argument for just a minute or two as to how she was a married woman at the time, an adulteress in fact, and certainly not unknowing in the ways of carnal life, but that didn't hold water, apparently. She was excused and taken back to the loony bin and put back in her hanging gray frock and slippers and that was it for the real world. She heard that Phil pulled eighteen months in the state prison. She couldn't sympathize, being in one of her own.

Jolene didn't think much about Mickey, but she drew his face over and over. She drew headstones in a graveyard and then drew his face on the gravestones. This seemed to her a worthy artistic task. The more she drew of Mickey the more she remembered the details of how he looked out at her on the last evening of his life, but it was hard with just crayons – they would only give her crayons to draw with, not the colored pencils she asked for.

Then something good happened. One of the girls in the ward smashed the mirror over the sink in the bathroom and used a sliver of it to cut her wrists. Well, that of course wasn't good, but all the mirrors in the bathroom were removed and nobody could see herself except maybe if they stood on the bed and the sunlight was in the right place in the windows behind the mesh screen. So Jolene began a business in portraits. She drew a girl's face, and soon they were waiting in line to have her draw them. If they didn't have a mirror, they had Jolene. Some of her likenesses were not very good, but since in most cases they were a lot better than the originals, nobody minded. Mrs.

Ames, the head nurse, thought that was good therapy for everyone and so Jolene was given a set of watercolors with three brushes, and a big thick sketchpad, and when the rage for portraits had played itself out, she painted everything else – the ward, the game room, the yard where they walked, the flowers in the flowerbed, the sunset through the black mesh, everything.

But since she was as sane as anyone, she was more and more desperate to get out of there. After a year or so she made the best deal she could, with one of the night attendants, a sharp-faced woman sallow in coloring but decent and roughly kind to people, name of Cindy. Jolene thought Cindy, with the leathery lines in her face, might be no less than fifty years old. She had an eye for Jolene right from the beginning. She gave her cigarettes to smoke outside behind the garbage bins, and she knew hair and makeup. She said, Red – Jolene had what they call strawberry hair, so that of course was her nickname there – Red, you don't want to cover up those freckles. They are charming in a girl like you, they give your face a sunlight. And, see, if you keep pulling back your hair into ponytails your hairline will recede, so we'll cut it just a bit shorter so that it curls up as it wants to and we let it frame your sweet face and, lo and behold, you are as pretty as a picture.

Cindy liked the freckles on Jolene's breasts, too, and it wasn't too bad being loved up by a woman. It was not her first choice, but Jolene thought, Once you get going it doesn't matter who it is or what they've got – there is the same panic, after all, and we are blind at such moments. But anyway that was the deal, and though in order to get herself out of the loony bin she agreed to live with Cindy in her own home, where she would cuddle secretly like her love child, she did so only until she could escape from there as well. With just a couple of clicks of doorlocks, and some minutes of hiding in a supply closet, and then with more keys turning and a creak of gate swings, Jolene rode to freedom in the trunk of Cindy's beat-up Corolla. It was even easier, after one night, walking out Cindy's front door in broad daylight once the woman had gone back to work.

Jolene hit the road. She wanted out of that town and out of that county however she could. She had almost a hundred dollars from her watercolor business. She hitched some and rode some local buses. She had a small suitcase and a lot of attitude to get her safe across state lines. She worked in a five-and-ten in Lexington and an industrial laundry in Memphis. There was always a YWCA, to stay out of trouble. And while she did have to take a deep breath and sell it once or twice across the country, it had the virtue of hardening her up for her own protection. She was just seventeen by then but carrying herself with some new clothes like she was ten years older, so that nobody would know there was just this scared girl-child inside the hip slinger with the platform strap shoes.

Which brought her to Phoenix, Arizona, a hot flat city of the desert, but with a lot of fast-moving people who lived inside their air-conditioning.

*

She appreciated that in the West human society was less tight-assed, nobody cared that much what you did or who your parents were and most everyone you met came from somewhere else. Before long she was working at a Dairy Queen and had a best friend, Kendra, who was one of her roommates, a Northern girl from Akron, Ohio.

The Dairy Queen was at the edge of city life with a view over warehouses to the flat desert with its straight roads and brownish mountains away in the distance. She had to revert back to her real age to get this job. It involved roller-skating, a skill which she fortunately had not forgotten. You skated out to the customers with their order on a tray that you hooked to the car window. It was only minimum, but some men would give you a good tip, though women never did. And anyway that wasn't to last long, because this cute guy kept coming around every day. He had long hair, a scraggly lip beard, and a ring in his ear – he looked like a rock star. He wore an undershirt with his jeans and boots, so you could see the tattoos that went up and down his arms, across his shoulders, and onto his chest. He even had a guitar in the back of his 1965 plum Caddy convertible. Of course she ignored his entreaties, though he kept coming back, and if another girl waited on him he asked her where Jolene was. All the girls wore nametags, you see. One day he drove up, and when she came back with his order he was sitting on the top of the front seat with a big smile, though a front tooth was missing. He strummed his guitar and he said, Listen to this, Jolene, and he sang this song he had made up, and as he sang he laughed in appreciation, as if someone else was singing.

*Jolene, Jolene*
*She is so mean*
*She won't be seen with me*
*At the Dairy Queen.*

*Jolene, Jolene*
*Please don't be mean*
*Your name it means to me*
*My love you'll glean from me*
*I am so keen to see*
*How happy we will be*
*When you are one with me*
*Jolene, Jolene*
*My Dairy Queen*

Well, she knew he was a sly one, but he'd gone to the trouble of thinking it up, didn't he? The people in the next car laughed and applauded and she blushed right through her freckles, but she couldn't help laughing along with them. And of course with his voice not very good and his guitar not quite in tune, she knew he was no rock star, but he was loud and didn't mind making a fool of himself and she liked that.

In fact, the guy was by profession a tattoo artist. His name was Coco Leger, pronounced Lerjay. He was originally from New Orleans, and she did go out dancing with him the next Saturday, though her friend Kendra strongly advised against it. The guy is a sleaze, Kendra said. Jolene thought she might be right. On the other hand, Kendra had no boyfriend of her own at the moment. And she was critical about most everything – their jobs, what she ate, the movies they saw, the furniture that came with the rental apartment, and maybe even the city of Phoenix in its entirety.

But Jolene went on the date and Coco was almost a gentleman. He was a good disco dancer, though a bit of a showoff with all his pelvic moves, and what was the harm after all. Coco Leger made her laugh, and she hadn't had a reason to laugh in a long time.

One thing led to another. There was first a small heart to be embossed for free on her behind, and before long she was working as an apprentice at Coco's Institute of Body Art. He showed her how to go about things, and she caught on quick and eventually she got to doing customers who wanted the cheap stock tattoos. It was drawing with a needle, a slow process like using only the tip of your paintbrush one dab at a time. Coco was very impressed with how fast she learned. He said she was a real asset. He fired the woman who worked for him, and after a serious discussion Jolene agreed to move in with him in his two rooms above his store, or studio, as he called it.

Kendra, who was still at the Dairy Queen, sat and watched her pack her things. I can see what he sees in you, Jolene, she said. You've got a trim little figure and everything moves the way it should without your even trying. Thank you, Kendra. Your skin is so fair, Kendra said. And you've got that nose that turns up, and a killer smile. Thank you, Kendra, she said again, and gave her a hug because, though she was happy for herself, she was sad for Kendra, whose really pretty face would not be seen for what it was by most men in that she was a heavyset girl with fat on her shoulders who was not very graceful on skates. But, Kendra continued, I can't see what you see in him. This is a man born to betray.

Still, she didn't want to go back to skating for tips. Coco was teaching her a trade that suited her talents. But when after just a couple of weeks Coco decided they should get married, she admitted to herself she knew nothing about him, his past, his family. She knew nothing, and when she asked, he just laughed and said, Babe, I am an orphan in the storm, just like you. They didn't much like me where I come from, but as I understan', neither of us has a past to write home about, he said holding her and kissing her neck. What counts is this here moment, he whispered, and the future moments to come.

She said the name Jolene Leger, pronounced Lerjay, secretly to herself and thought it had a nice lilt to it. And so after another justice of the peace and a corsage in her hand and a flowered dress to her ankles and a bottle of champagne, she was in fact Jolene Leger, a married woman once again. They went back to the two rooms above the store and smoked dope and made love, with Coco sing-songing to her in her rhythm *Jolene Jolene she's a love machine*, and after he fell asleep and began to snore she got up and stood at the window and looked out on the street. It was three in the morning by then, but all the streetlights were on and the traffic signals were going, though not a human being was in sight. It was all busyness on that empty street in its silence, all the store signs blazing away, the neon colors in the windows, the laundromat, the check-cashing store, the one-hour photo and passport, the newsdealer, the coffee shop, and the dry cleaner's, and the parking meters looking made of gold under the amber light of the street lamps. It was the world going on as if people were the last thing it needed or wanted.

She found herself thinking that if you shaved off Coco's scraggly lip beard and if his tattoos could be scrubbed away, and you took off his boots with the lifts in them and got him a haircut and maybe set a pair of eyeglasses on his nose, he would look not unlike her first husband, the late Mickey Holler, and she began to cry.

For a while she was sympathetic to Coco's ways and wanted to believe his stories. But it became more and more difficult. He was away in his damn car half the time, leaving her to man the shop as if he didn't care what business they lost. He kept all moneys to himself. She realized she was working without a salary, which only a wife would do – who else would stand for that? It was a kind of slavery, wasn't it? Which is what Kendra said, tactlessly, when she came to visit. Coco was critical of most everything Jolene did or said. And when she needed money for groceries or some such he would only reluctantly peel off a bill or two from his carefully hoarded wad. She began to wonder where he got all his cash – certainly not from the tattooing trade, which was not all that great once the dry, cold Arizona winter set in. And when a reasonable-looking woman did come in, he carried on saying all sorts of suggestive things as if they were the only two people in the room. I really don't like that, Jolene told him. Not at all. You married yourself a good-lookin' stud, Coco said. Get used to it. And when Jolene found herself doing a snake or a whiskered fish for some muscleman, and, as you'd expect working so closeup, he'd come on to her, all Coco could say when she complained was, That's what makes the world go roun'. She became miserable on a daily basis. The drugs he was dealing took up more and more of his time and when she confronted him he didn't deny it. In fact, he said, it was the only way to keep the shop going. You should know without I have to tell you, Jolene, no artist in this USA can make it he don't have somethin' on the side.

One day a taxicab pulled up and a woman carrying a baby and holding a valise came into the store. She was a blonde, very tall, statuesque even, and although the sign was clearly printed on the store window, she said, Is this the Institute of Body Art of which Coco Leger is the proprietor? Jolene nodded. I would like to see him, please, the woman said, putting the valise down and shifting the baby from one arm to the other. She looked about thirty or thirty-five and she was wearing a hat, and had just a linen jacket and a yellow dress with hose and shoes, which was most unusual on this winter day in Phoenix, or in any season of the year for that matter, where you didn't see anyone who wasn't wearing jeans. Jolene had the weirdest feeling come over her. She felt that she was a child again. She was back in childhood – she'd only been a pretend adult and was not Mrs. Coco Leger except in her stupid dreams. It was a premonition. She looked again at the baby and at that moment knew what she didn't have to be told. Its ancestry was written all over its runty face. All it lacked was a little lip beard.

And you are? Jolene asked. I am Marin Leger, the wife of that fucking son of a bitch, the woman said.

As if any confirmation was needed, her large hand coming around from under the baby's bottom had a gold band impressed into the flesh of its fourth finger.

I have spent every cent I had tracking him down and I want to see him now, this very instant, the woman said. A moment later, as if a powerful magic had been invoked, Coco's Caddy rolled to the curb and it may have been worth everything to see the stunned expression on his face as he got out of the car and both saw Marin Leger and was seen by her through the shop window. But, being Coco, he recovered nicely. His face lit up and he waved as if he couldn't have been more delighted. And came through the door with a grin. Looka this, he said. Will ya looka this! he said, his arms spread wide. Because she was the taller of the two, the hug he gave her mashed his face against the baby in her arms, who commenced to cry loudly. And as Coco stepped back he suffered the free hand of the woman smartly against his cheek.

Now, darlin', just be calm, he told her, stay calm. There is an esplanation for everthin'. Come with me, we have to talk, he said to her, as if he'd been waiting for her all along. Believe it or not I am greatly relieved to see you, he said to her. He took no further notice of the kid in her arms, and as he picked up her bag and ushered her out the door, he looked back at Jolene and told her out of the side of his mouth to hold tight, to hold tight, and outside he gallantly opened the car door for Marin Leger and sat her and their baby down and went off with them in the plum-color Caddy 1965 convertible he had once driven up every day to see Jolene wiggle her ass on skates.

*Jolene, Jolene, of the Dairy Queen, she is so mean, she smashed the machinery* . . . She had never been so calm in her life as she quietly and methodically trashed the Leger Institute of Body Art, turning over the autoclave, pulling down the flash posters, banging the tattoo guns by their cables against the rear exposed brick wall until they cracked, scattering the needle bars, pouring the inks on the floor, pulling the display case of 316L stainless-steel body jewelry off the wall, tearing the paperback tattoo books in the rotating stand. She smashed the director's chairs to pieces and threw a metal footstool through the backdoor window. She went upstairs and, suddenly aware for the first time how their rooms smelled of his disgusting unwashed body, she busted up everything she could, tore up the bedding, swept everything out of the medicine cabinet, and pulled down the curtains she had chosen to make the place more homey. She took an armful of her clothes and stuffed them into two paper sacks and when she found in a shoebox on their closet shelf a Ziploc plastic bag with another inside it packed with white stuff that felt under the thumb like baking powder, she left it exactly where it was and, downstairs again, cleaned out the few dollars that were in the cash register, picked up the phone, left a precise message for the Phoenix PD, and, putting up the BACK IN FIVE sign, she slammed the door behind her and was gone.

She was still dry-eyed when she went to the pawnshop two blocks away and got fifteen dollars for her wedding band. She waited at the storefront travel agency where the buses stopped and didn't begin to cry till she wondered, for the first time in a long time, who her mom and dad might have been and if they were still alive as she thought they must be if they were too young to do anything but name her Jolene and leave her for the authorities to raise.


In Vegas she waitressed at a coffee shop till she had enough money to have her hair straightened, which is what the impresario of the Starlet Topless told her she had to do if she wanted a job. So if she shook her head as she leaned back holding on to the brass pole, her hair swished back and forth across her shoulders. Wearing a thong and high heels was not the most comfortable thing in the world, but she got the idea of things quickly enough and became popular as the most petite girl in the place. The other girls liked her, too – they called her Baby and watched out for her. She rented a room in the apartment of a couple of them. Even the bouncer was solicitous after she lied to him that she was involved.

When she met Sal, a distinguished gray-haired man of some girth, it was at the request of the manager, who took her to a table in the back. That this man Sal chose not to sit at the bar and stare up her ass suggested to her he was not the usual bum who came into Starlet's. He was a gentleman who though not married had several grandchildren. The first thing he did on their first date when she came up to his penthouse suite was show her their pictures. That's the kind of solid citizen Mr. Sal Fontaine was. She stood at the window looking out over all of Vegas. Quiet and soft-spoken Sal was not only a dear man, as she came to know him, but one highly respected as the founder and owner of Sal's Line, with an office and banks of phones with operators taking calls from people all over the country wanting Sal's Line on everything from horses to who would be the next President. Without ceremony, which was his way, he put a diamond choker on her neck and asked her to move in with him. She couldn't believe her luck, living with a man highly regarded in the community in his penthouse suite of six rooms overlooking all of Vegas. It had maid service every morning. From the French restaurant downstairs you could order dinner on a rolling cart that turned into a table. Sal bought her clothes, she signed his name at the beauty parlor, and when they went out, though he was so busy it was not that often, she was treated with respect by the greeters, and by Sal's associates, mostly gentlemen of the same age range as his. She was totally overwhelmed. With all the leggy ass in Las Vegas, imagine, little Jolene, treated like a princess! And not only that but with time on her hands to develop a line of her own, of greeting cards she drew, psychedelic in style, sometimes inspired by her experience with tattoo designs but always with the sentiments of loving family relationships that she dreamed up, as if she knew all about it.

She never thought she could be so happy. Sal liked her to climb all over him, he liked her to be on top, and they were very tender and caressing of one another, certainly on her part, because always in the back of her mind was the fear of his overexerting himself. And he talked so quietly, and he believed or pretended to believe her life story – the parts that were made up as well as the parts that were true.

As she became used to the life, she reflected that Sal Fontaine did not give of himself easily. It wasn't a matter of his material generosity. He never confided in her. There was a distance in him, or maybe even a gloom, that for all his success he could not change in himself. If she had questions, if she was curious, she met a wall. He moved slowly, as if the air set up a resistance just to him. When he smiled it was a sad smile despite his capped teeth. And he had heavy jowls and hooded sad eyes made darker by the deep blue pouches under them. Maybe he could not forget what

93

he had lost, his old country or his original family, who was she to say?

She would tell him she loved him, and at the moment she said it, she did. The rest of the time she sort of shrugged to herself. The contractual nature of their relationship was all too clear to her, and she began to suspect that the regard Sal's friends held for her was not what they might have expressed among themselves. Her life, once the novelty wore off, was like eating cotton candy all day long. Her long straight red hair now shone with highlights. In the mornings she would swim in the hotel Olympic-size pool with her hair in a single braid, trailing. She was this Jolene person who wore different Vegas-style outfits depending on the time of day or night. She saw herself in an I. Magnin fitting-room mirror one day and the word that came to her mind was *hard*. When had it happened that she'd taken on that set of the mouth and stony gaze of the Las Vegas bimbo? Jesus.

One evening they were sitting watching television and Sal said, out of the blue, that she didn't have to worry, she would be taken care of, he would settle something on her. Thank you, sweetheart, she said, not knowing exactly how or when he would do that but understanding the essential meaning – that she was in a situation designed not to last. The next morning she took all her greeting-card designs to a print shop at the edge of town and spent two hours making decisions about the stock she wanted, the layouts, the typefaces, the amounts to print of each item, and so on. It was real business and it made her feel good, even though she had no idea of who would distribute her cards let alone who would buy them. Step by step, she told herself in the cab back. Step by step.

A week later the phone rang just when they were getting up and Sal told her quickly to get dressed and go have breakfast in the coffee shop because some men were coming for a meeting. She said that was okay, she would stay out of the way in the bedroom with a cup of coffee and the *Sun*. Don't argue, he shouted, and threw a dress at her face. She was speechless – he had never yelled at her before. She was waiting for the elevator when the doors opened and they came out, the men to meet with Sal. She saw them and they saw her, two of them looking, like so many of the men in Vegas, as if they had never felt the sun on their face.

But then in the coffee shop it dawned on her. She all at once turned cold and then sick to her stomach. She ran to the ladies' and sat there in a cold sweat. Such stories as you heard were never supposed to intrude into your own life.

How long did she sit there? When she found the courage to come out, and then out of the coffee shop into the lobby, she saw an ambulance at the front entrance. She stood in the crowd that gathered and saw the elevator doors open and someone with an oxygen mask over his face and hooked up to an intravenous line being wheeled on a gurney through the lobby.

That it was Sal Fontaine was quickly agreed upon by everyone.

Exactly what had happened to him was less clear.

Finally, a police officer walking by said it was a heart attack. A heart attack.

She did not even have her purse, just the orange print mini she wore and the sandals. She didn't even have any makeup – she had nothing. She saw the name of the hospital on the ambulance as it drove off and decided to go upstairs and put something on and take a cab there. But she couldn't move. She walked up the winding staircase to the mezzanine and sat there in an armchair with her hands between her knees. Finally, she got up the courage to go back to the penthouse floor. If it was a heart attack, what were the police and TV cameras doing there? Everyone in the world was in the corridor, and the door to the apartment was sealed with yellow tape and under guard and everything was out of her reach – Mr. Sal Fontaine, and all her clothes, and her diamond choker, and even the money he had given her over time, despite the fact that he never allowed her to pay for anything.

She had over a thousand dollars in the drawer on her side of the bed. She knew that eventually she could reclaim it if she wanted to be questioned by the police. But whatever was to happen to her now might not be as bad as what would happen if she risked it. Even if she told them nothing, what would Sal's Line be on the chances of her living to her nineteenth birthday, which happened also to be the next day? He was not around to tell her.

Which is how life changes, as lightning strikes, and in an instant what was is not what is and you find yourself sitting on a rock at the edge of the desert, hoping some bus will come by and take pity on you before you're found lying dead there like any other piece of road kill.


Two years later, Jolene was living alone in Tulsa, Oklahoma. She had heard from a truck driver at a whistle stop in north Texas, where she was waiting tables, that Tulsa was a boomtown with not enough people for all the jobs. She'd taken a room at a women's residential hotel and first found work, part-time, in the public library shelving books and then full-time as a receptionist at a firm that leased oil-drilling equipment. She had not been with anyone in a while, but it was kind of nice actually. She was surprised at how pleasant life could be when you were on your own. She liked the way she felt walking in the street or sitting at a desk. Self-contained. Nothing begging inside her. I have come of age, she told herself. I have come of age.

To make some extra cash, she worked after hours on a call basis for a caterer. She had to invest in the uniform – white blouse, black trousers, and black pumps – but each time she was called it meant sixty dollars, for a minimum three hours. She wore her hair in the single braid down her back and she kept her eyes lowered as instructed but, even so, managed to see a good deal of the upper crust of Tulsa.

She was serving champagne on a tray at a private party one evening when this six-footer with blow-dried hair appeared before her. He was good-looking and he knew it.

He grabbed a glass of champagne, drank it off, took another, and followed her into the kitchen. He didn't get anything out of her but her name, but he tracked her down through the caterer and sent her flowers with a note, signed Brad G. Benton, asking her out to dinner. Nobody in all her life had ever done that.

So she bought herself a dress and went out to dinner with Brad G. Benton at the country club, where the table linen was starched and there were crystal wineglasses and padded red leather chairs with brass studs. She wouldn't remember what she ate. She sat and listened with her hands in her lap. She didn't have to say much; he did all the talking. Brad G. Benton was not thirty-five and already a senior V.P. at this stock brokerage where they kept on giving him bonuses. He didn't want just to get her in bed. He said since Jesus had come into his heart, the only really good sex remaining to him was connubial sex. He said, Of course you need someone precious and special enough for that, like you, Jolene, and looked deeply into her eyes.

At first, she couldn't believe he was serious. After a couple of more dates she realized he was. She was thinking Brad G. Benton must be crazy. On the other hand, this was the Bible Belt – she had seen these super-sincere people at her receptionist's job. They might be rich and do sophisticated business around the world, but they were true believers in God's written word, with no ifs, ands, or buts. From the looks of things it was a knockout combination, though a little weird, like they had one foot in the boardroom and one in heaven.

You don't know anything about me, Jolene told him in an effort to satisfy herself of her integrity. I expect soon to know everything, he said flashing a big handsome smile that could have been a leer.

He was so damn cocky. She almost resented that there was never any doubt in his mind as to what she would say. He insisted she quit her job and move to a hotel at his expense until the wedding day. Oh, what day is that? she said, teasing, but he was a wild man: The engagement will necessarily be short, he said, slipping a diamond ring on her finger.

A week later they were married in the chapel of the First Methodist church there in Tulsa that looked like Winchester Cathedral. Brad G. Benton brought her to live in his apartment in a new building that had a swimming pool in the basement and a gym on the roof. They were high enough to see out over the whole city, though there wasn't that much to see in Tulsa, Oklahoma.

So once more her fortunes had changed and little Jolene was a young matron of the upper class. She wanted to write to someone about this incredible turn in her life, but who could she write to? Who? There was no one. In that sense nothing had changed, because she was as alone as she had always been, a stranger in a strange land.

Things in the marriage were okay at first, though some of Brad G. Benton's ideas were not to her taste. He was very athletic and no sooner satisfied in one orifice than she was turned over for the other. Also, he seemed not to notice her artwork. She had bought an easel and set up a little studio in what was designed to be the maid's room, because the Indian woman who cooked and cleaned had her own home to go to each evening. Jolene painted there and stretched her canvas, and she took a figure-painting class once a week where there were live models. She did well, her teacher was very encouraging, but Brad took none of this in. He just didn't notice – he was too busy with his work and his workouts and his nights out and his nights in her.

It turned out that Brad G. Benton's family was prominent in Tulsa. Not one of them had come to the wedding, their purpose being to define to her what white trash meant. At first she didn't care that much. But she'd see their pictures in the newspapers being honored at charity events. They had wings of buildings named after them. One day, coming from shopping, she looked out of the cab window as it passed a glass office tower that said BENTON INTERNATIONAL on a giant brass cube balanced on one of its corners in the plaza out front.

She said to Brad, I would think they had more respect for you if not for me. But he only laughed. It was not so much that he was a democrat in his ideals, as she was to realize, it was part of his life's work to do outrageous things and raise hell. It was how he kept everyone's attention. He loved to twist noses out of joint. He was contrary. He hadn't joined the Benton family enterprise as he was supposed to – it was a holding company with many different kinds of business in their hands – but had gone off on his own to show what he was made of.

Jolene knew that if she wanted to prove anything to his family, if she wanted any kind of social acceptance in Tulsa, Oklahoma, she would have to work for it. She would have to start reading books and take a course or two in something intellectual and embrace the style of life, the manners, the ways of doing and talking by being patient and keeping her eyes and ears open. She would attend their church, too. As wild as he was, Brad was like his father, what he called a strong Christian. That was the one place they would have to meet and, she was willing to bet, speak to one another. And how then could the family not speak to her?

Oddly enough, she was looking as good as she ever had, and Brad took her once a week to dinner at the country club to show her off. By then everyone in town knew this so-called Cinderella story. Grist for the mill. He was heedless. He just didn't worry about it, whereas she could hardly raise her head. One evening, his father and mother were sitting at a far table with their guests, who looked as if they were there to serve them no less than the waiters. Brad waved – it was more like a salute – and the father nodded and resumed his conversation.

Through no fault of her own Jolene had stepped into a situation that was making her life miserable. Whatever was going on with these people, what did it have to do with her? Nothing. She was as nothing.

To tell the truth, she had made Brad for a creep that first time he came on to her at that cocktail party. He'd padded into the kitchen, stalking her like some animal, taken the empty champagne tray out of her hands, and told her redheads smelled different. And he stood there sniffing her and going, Hmmm, yes, like warm milk.

After the baby was born, when Brad G. Benton started to bat her around, Jolene could not help but remember that first impression. Every little thing drove him crazy. It got so she couldn't do anything, say anything, without he would go off half-cocked. He took to hitting her, slapping her face, punching her. What are you doing? she screamed. Stop it, stop it! It was his new way of getting off. He would say, You like this? You like it? He'd knock her around, then push her down on the bed. She grew accustomed to living in fear of getting beaten up and forced against her will. She was still to learn what they would teach at the shelter – it happens once, that's it, you leave. But now she just tried to see it through. Brad G. Benton had been to college, he came of money and he wore good clothes, and she was flattered that he would fall for her when she hadn't even a high school diploma. And then of course there were the apologies and the beggings for forgiveness and the praying in church together, and by such means she slowly became a routinely abused wife.

Only when it was all over would she realize it wasn't just having the baby; it was their plans for him, the Bentons' plans for her Mr. Nipplebee. He was an heir, after all. The minute they'd found out she was pregnant, they went to work. And after he was born, they slowly gave it to Brad in bits and pieces, what their investigators had learned about her life before. Never mind that she had tried to tell Brad about her marriages, her life on the road. He never wanted to hear it; he had no curiosity about her – none. She had appeared in Tulsa as a vision, God's chosen sex partner for him, a fresh and wet and shining virgin with red hair. All those beatings were what he was told, and all those apologies were the way his love for her was hanging on. She would feel sorry for him if she could because he was so wired, such a maniac. It was as if his wildness, his independent choice of life, was being driven from him, as if it was the Devil. It was those parents slowly absorbing him back into their righteousness.

One day Brad G. Benton appeared at the door to her little studio room when he ordinarily would be at work. She was ruling off a grid on one of her canvases as she had been taught. Brad! she said, smiling, but there was no recognition in his eyes. He kicked the stool out from under her. He broke the easel over his knee, he bashed her canvases against the wall, tore down the drawings she had pinned up there, and then he squeezed tubes of paint into her face as he held her down on the floor. And he began hitting her as she lay there. He punched her face, he punched her in the throat. When he got off her, she could hear his breathing – it was like crying. He stood over her, kicked her in the side, and as suddenly as he had come he was gone.

She lay there moaning in pain, too frightened and shocked even to get up until she thought of the baby. She dragged herself to the nursery. The Cherokee woman who had heard everything sat beside the crib with her hand over her eyes. But the baby was sleeping peacefully. Jolene washed her face and, wrapping up her Mr. Nipplebee, she took him with her as she dragged herself to a doctor. She was told that she had had her cheek fractured, two broken ribs, contusions of the throat, and a bruised kidney. How did this happen? the doctor asked her. She was afraid to tell him, and, besides, it hurt too much to talk. But the nurse in the office didn't have to be told. She wrote out the name and address of a women's shelter and said, Go there right now. I'll order you a cab. And in that way, with her precious in her arms and only what she wore, Jolene left her marriage.

She could hardly bear staying at the shelter, where there were these wimpy women looking for her friendship, her companionship. Jolene wouldn't even go to the group sessions. She stayed by herself and nursed Mr. Nipplebee.

The shelter gave her the name of a woman lawyer and she put down a retainer. Get me a divorce as fast as you can, she told the lawyer. The money – I don't care, I'll take anything they give. I just want out of here and out of Tulsa, Oklahoma. And then she waited, and waited, and nothing happened. Absolutely nothing. This went on for some time. And the next thing Jolene knew, when she was about strapped of her savings account, the lawyer quit on her. She was an older woman who wore pinstripe suits and big loopy bronze earrings. I may be broke, Jolene said to her, but Brad G. Benton has money to burn and I can pay you afterwards out of the alimony or child care.

You didn't tell me you had a past including a stretch in juvenile detention, the lawyer said. To say nothing of a previous as yet unannulled marriage to a convicted drug dealer.

Jolene was so stunned she didn't think to ask how the lawyer knew that if she hadn't told her.

She was up against a scumbag husband on his own turf, so what could she expect but that there was worse to come, as there was, if he knew all along where she was hiding, and if he knew by first names everyone in town, as he probably did the very police officers who came one morning to arrest her for unlawful kidnapping of her own child, who they took from her arms and drove off in one squad car with Jolene in another as she looked back screaming.

I don't want to hear about what is the law in this country and what is not, Jolene told the Legal Aid person who was assigned to her. Do you know what it means to have your child torn from you? Do you have to have that happen to you to know that it is worse than death? Because though you want to kill yourself, you cannot have that relief for thinking of the child's welfare in the hands of a sick father who never smiled at him and was jealous of him from the day he was born.

My baby, she said aloud when she was alone. My baby.

He had her coloring and button nose and carrot-red fuzz for hair. He drank from her with a born knowledge of what was expected of him. He was a whole new life in her arms, and for the very first time she could remember she

105

had something she wanted. She was Jolene, his mother, and could believe in God now, who had never before seemed to her to be much of a fact of life.

And so now there was a hearing for the divorce Brad had filed for. And his whole miserable family was there – they loved him after all now that he was getting rid of her and her past was thrown in her face. They had it all down, including the medical records of her STD from Coco, her living in sin, and even her suspension one term at South Sumter High for smoking pot. It was a no-brainer, her Legal Aid kid was out of his league, and without giving it much thought, the judge ruled she was an unfit mother and granted Brad G. Benton sole custody of her Mr. Nipplebee.

On top of everything, in the fullness of her milk that she had to pump out, she must have done something wrong, because she ended up in the hospital with a staph infection that had to be drained, like the milk had gone bad and turned green. But she had a chance to think. She thought of her choices. She could kill Brad G. Benton – it'd be simple enough to buy some kind of gun and wait on him – but then the baby would be raised by the Benton family. So what was the point? She could find a job and see the baby every second Sunday for one hour, as allowed by the judge, and rely on the passing of time for the moment when nobody would be looking and she could steal him back and run for it. But then on her first visitation what happened was that Brad was up in the gym and a new large Indian woman was with Mr. Nipplebee, and Brad's crone of a mother stood with her back to the door and they wouldn't let Jolene hold him but just sit by the crib and watch him sleep. And she thought, If I stay on in Tulsa for my visitations, he will grow up learning to think of me as an embarrassment, a poor relation, and I can't have that.

These days, Jolene has this job in West Hollywood inking for a small comic-book company, except they don't call them comic books – they call them graphic novels. Because most of them aren't funny at all. They are very serious. She likes the people at work, they are all good pals and go out for pizza together. But where she lives is down near the farmers' market, in a studio apartment that is sacred to her. Nobody can come in no matter how good a friend. She has a little stereo for her Keith Jarrett CDs and she lights a candle and drinks a little wine and dreams of plans for herself. She thinks someday, when she has more ex- perience, of writing a graphic novel of her own, *The Life of Jolene*.

She has a pastel sketch she once did of her precious baby. It is so sweet! It's the only likeness she has. Sometimes she looks at this sketch and then at her own face in the mirror, and because he takes after her in his col- oring and features, she tries to draw him at what he might look like at his present age, which is four and a half.

Friends tell Jolene she could act in movies because she may be twenty-five but she looks a lot younger. And they like her voice that she has courtesy of her ex-husband, the way it cracks like Janis Joplin's. And her crooked smile, which she doesn't tell them is the result of a busted cheekbone. So she's had some photos taken and is sending them out to professional agents.

I mean, why not? Jolene says to herself. Her son could see her up on the screen one day? And when she took herself back to Tulsa in her Rolls-Royce automobile he would answer the door and there would be his movie-star mother.

# WALTER JOHN HARMON

When Betty told me she would go that night to Walter John Harmon, I didn't think I reacted. But she looked into my eyes and must have seen something – some slight loss of vitality, a moment's dullness of expression. And she understood that for all my study and hard work, the Seventh Attainment was still not mine.

Dearest, she said, don't be discouraged. The men have more difficulty. Walter John Harmon knows that and commends your struggle. You can go see him if you wish, it is the prerogative of husbands.

No, I said, I'm all right.

After she had gone I went walking in the evening light across the pastures. It is beautiful country here, a broad undulant valley with brooks and natural ponds and no ground light to dim the stars or the moving lights of the jets up among them. This is where the Holy City will descend. The community has in just two short years

111

assembled the parcels of this valley. I did some real estate law back in Charlotte and I am proud to say I have had no small hand in our accomplishment. It is in the nature of a miracle that Walter John Harmon has in his effortless way drawn so many of us to his prophecy. And that we have given everything we possess – not to him, to the Demand that comes through him. We are not idiots. We are not cult victims. In many quarters we are laughed at for following as God's prophet a garage mechanic who in his teens was imprisoned for car theft. But this blessed man has revolutionized our lives. From the first moment I was in his presence I felt resolved in my soul. Everything was suddenly right. I was who I was. It is hard to explain. I saw the outside world darkened, as in a film negative. But I was in the light. And that I was blessed seemed to be established in his eyes. Walter's pale blue eyes are set so deep under the ridge of his brow that the irises are occluded at the top, like half moons. It is almost a chilling gaze you feel on you, as gentle as it may be, something not of this world but ineffable, expressive of God, like the gaze of an animal.

So I knew the failing within me when Betty was this night summoned for Purification. Walter is at a level beyond lust. This is apparent, since all the wives, even the plainest, partake of his communion. His ministry annuls the fornications of a secular society. Betty and I, for example, made love many times before we were married. And the Community's children, the children in white, who have never known carnal sin, are not permitted to look at Walter John Harmon lest he inspire them to their confusion. They are the precious virgins, girls and boys, whose singing brings him such joy. He says nothing to them, of course, but smiles and closes those remarkable eyes, and the tears stream from them like rain down a windowpane.

Betty and I learned about Walter John Harmon from the Internet. I found myself reading someone's Web log – how that happened I can't remember. I think of it now as the beginning of His summons, for there is nothing without significance in this world made by God. I called Betty and she came into my study and together we read of this most remarkable event of the tornado that had occurred the year before in the town of Fremont in west Kansas. There were links, too, all from this locality and all telling the same story. I logged in to the archives of the regional newspapers and confirmed that there had been a series of tornados all through the state at that time, and a particularly destructive twister that had hit Fremont head-on. But beyond that not one news report had the key thing. Not even in the Fremont *Sun-Ledger* was there an account of this one inexplicable occurrence of the cyclone that came through the middle of town, flinging cars into the air, shattering storefronts, lifting houses off their foundations and, among other disasters, setting off a gas-and-oil fire that pooled on the floor of the repair shop of the Getty station on the corner of Railroad and Division Streets, where Walter John Harmon worked as a mechanic.

I hold in my mind a composite account of what

happened, from the Web logs and from what we have since heard recounted by the townspeople who witnessed this or that particular moment and who followed Walter in his ministry and are now the Community Elders. Walter John Harmon himself has not been persuaded to write down a testament, nor has he permitted anything to be written in the way of documentation. "It is not the time for that," he says. And then, "May it never be the time, for the day we falter and lose our way, that will be the time." In fact nothing in the Community is written. The Ideals, the Imperatives, the Assignments and Obligations are all pronounced, and once spoken by the prophet are carried and remembered by means of daily prayer. The miracles of the tornado are held in the imaginations of our minds and we speak of them to one another in our workday or social gatherings, so that as the years pass there will be a Consensus of the inner truth and its authority will be unquestionable.

As he stood by the pool of fire, the garage doors first, and then the roof and then the collapsed walls, were lifted and spun into the black funnel. Only Walter John Harmon stood where he stood, and then was slowly raised in his standing and turned slowly in his turning, calmly and silently, his arms stretched wide in the black shrieking, with the things of our lives whirling in the whirlwind above him – car fenders and machines from the laundromat, hats and empty coats and trousers, tables, mattresses, plates and knives and forks, TV sets and computers, all malignantly alive in the black howling. And then a child flew into Walter John Harmon's left arm and another fell into his right arm, and he held them steadfast and was lowered to the ground where he had stood. And then the dreaded wind that takes all breath away was gone, having blown itself to bits. And the fields beyond the town were strewn with the several dead and dying among their possessions. But the pool of fire in the Getty garage was nothing but a ring of blackened concrete, and the sun was out as if the tornado had never been, and the mothers of those two children came running and found them bruised and bleeding and crying but alive. Only then did Walter John Harmon begin again to breathe, though he stood where he stood, unable to move as if in a trance, until he collapsed and lost consciousness.

All of this is in the Consensus. Other elements of the miracle are still debated by the Community and I suppose come under the heading of apocrypha. One of the Elders, Ansel Bernes, who had owned a clothing store, claims that seven mercury street lamps on the walking street in the Fremont business district came on and stayed on when the tornado hit. I can't quite accept this. According to the *Sun-Ledger*, Fremont's power outage was total. It took the local utility two days to get everyone back online.

When we came here Betty and I had been married a dozen years with no children to show for it. One of the appeals of the Community is that we are all parents of all children. While the adults live in distinct quarters of their own, as in the outer world, the children room together in the main house. At present we are a hundred ten in number, with a human treasury of seventy-eight children, ranging in age from two to fifteen.

Except for the main house, which was once a retreat for elderly nuns of the Roman Catholic persuasion and to which we have added a new wing, all the Community buildings were built by members according to the specifications of Walter John Harmon. He called for square, box-like structures with gable roofs for the adult houses, each of which contains two apartments of two rooms each. His own residence is slightly larger, with a gambrel roof, which gives it the appearance of a barn. All buildings in the complex are painted white; no colors are permitted exterior or interior. Metal fixtures are not allowed – window frames are wood, all water is drawn by hand from wells, there is no indoor plumbing, and communal showers, men's and women's, are jerry-rigged in tents. Walter John Harmon has said: "We praise what is temporary, we cherish the impermanent, for there can be no comparison with what is coming that is not an impiety."

But in the business suite in the new wing of the main house we do have computers, faxes, copiers, and so on, powered by a gasoline generator behind the building, though we intend when it is practical to switch to solar cells. There are metal filing cabinets as well. All of this is by dispensation because, regrettably, we do have necessary business with the outside world. We handle legal challenges from state and county officials and must deal also with private suits brought by unthinking or opportunistic relations of our family members. But only the Community lawyers, and Elder Rafael Altman, our financial officer and CPA, and his bookkeepers, and the women who provide clerical help, can enter these premises. Three of us practice law, and after morning prayers we go to work just like everyone else. By dispensation we own the habiliments of the legal profession – suits, shirts, ties, polished shoes, which we don for those occasions when we must meet with our counterparts in the world outside. We are driven by horse and wagon to the Gate down at the paved road some two miles away. There we have the choice of the three parked SUVs, though never the Hummer. The Hummer is reserved for Walter John Harmon. He does not proselytize, but he does schedule spiritual meetings on the outside. Or he will attend ecumenical or scholarly conferences on this or that religious or social issue. He is never invited to participate but is eloquent enough sitting quietly in the audience in his robe, his head bowed, his face almost hidden in the fall of his hair and his hands folded under his chin.

Betty returned early the next morning, the sun coming with her through the door, and I welcomed her with a hug. I meant it, too  I love seeing her face in the morning. She is very fair and rises from her sleep with her cheeks flushed like a child's and her hazel eyes instantly alert to the day. She is as lithe and fit as she was when she played field hockey at college. If you look closely some tiny lines radiate from the corners of her eyes, but this only makes her more attractive to me. Her hair is still the color of wheat and she still wears it short, as she did when I met her, and she still has that spring to her step and her typically energetic way of doing things.

We prayed together and then we had our bread and tea, chatting all the while. Betty served as a Community teacher, she had the kindergarten, and she was talking about her day's plan. I was feeling better. It was a beautiful day dawning with coverlets of white webbing on the grass. I had a renewed confidence in my own feelings.

All at once the most hideous carnal images arose in my mind. I wanted to speak but could not catch my breath.

What is it, Jim, what?

Betty held my hand. I closed my eyes until the images disappeared and I could breathe again.

Oh my dear one, she said. Last night was not the first time, after all. And have our lives changed? I'm telling you it is not a normal human experience with any of the normal results.

I don't want to hear about it. It is not necessary for me to hear about it.

It is no more, or no less, than a sacrament. It is no more than when the priest placed the wafer on our tongues.

I held my hand up. Betty looked at me inquiringly, as in the old days, a pretty bird with its head cocked, wondering who I could possibly be.

You know, she said, I had to tell Walter John Harmon. You should go see him. Look how your mouth is set, so hard, so angry.

It was not for you to tell him, I said.

I recognized an Obligation.

Outside in the sun, I breathed the sweet air of the valley and tried to calm myself. Everything around me was the vision of serene life. We are the quietest people. You will never hear a loud argument or see a public display of temperament anywhere in the Community.

Our children never fight, or push each other, or band together in hurtful cliques the way children do. The muslin we wear that suggests our common priesthood quiets the heart. The prayers we utter, the food we grow for ourselves in our fields, provide an immense and recurring satisfaction.

Betty followed me. Please, Jim, she said. You should talk to him. He will see you.

Yes? And what if I am excused from my work, if I am remanded, who can argue the case?

What case is that?

You're not entrusted to know. But believe me it's critical. He will not remand you then.

How can you know that? I may not be an Elder, but I'm approved to go beyond the Gate. And doesn't that presuppose the Seventh?

Why was I having to defend myself? Please, I said, I won't talk about this anymore.

Betty turned from me and I felt her coldness. I had the maniacal thought that the Purifications wouldn't be a problem for me if I no longer loved my wife.

At our supper at the end of the day she asked me to do

119

something, some minor chore that I would have done without her asking, and I thought her tone was officious.

To what extent was my legal work in the outside world holding me back from the prophetic realization offered by Walter John Harmon? Didn't I have one foot in and one foot out? But wasn't that my Imperative? He himself had said the higher Attainments are elusive, difficult, and, as if they had personalities of their own, they were given to teasing us with simulacra of themselves. So there was no shame in being remanded. Perhaps for my own sake I should have requested it. But then would I not be putting myself before the needs of the Community? And wouldn't that be to relinquish the Sixth Attainment?

The following morning before work I went to the Tabernacle to pray.

Our Tabernacle is no more than a lean-to. It stands at the high end of the lawn bordering the apple orchard. On a wooden table of our own making and without any ornamentation or covering sits a white stone and a common latchkey. I knelt in the grass in the sun with my head bowed and my hands clasped. But even as I uttered the prayers my mind split in two. As I mouthed the words all I could think of was this question: Had I come to the Community from the needs of my own heart, or had I deceived myself by taking for my own the convictions of my wife? That's how badly the doubts were assailing me.

When I looked up Walter John Harmon was standing in

the Tabernacle. I had not seen him approach. Nor was he looking at me. He was staring at the ground, seeing nothing but his own thoughts.

Walter does not deliver sermons because, as he maintains, we are not a church, we are an Unfolding Revelation. He will appear at the Tabernacle unannounced, any time of the day, any day of the week, as the spirit moves him. At such times, the word goes out and the members who can manage it run to hear him, and those whose work prevents this will hear his words later as committed to memory of those in attendance.

People came running now. Because Walter John Harmon is so soft-spoken it became apparent to the Elders at one point that a dispensation had to be made for a wireless microphone and a loudspeaker. As he stood in the Tabernacle in his characteristic way, with the fingertips of one hand touching the wooden table, and as he began to speak as he would have even if there were no one to listen, someone arrived with the speaker and set up the microphone on a stand in front of him. Even amplified, the prophet's voice was barely more than a whisper. There was such a diffidence about him, for as he had told us more than once, his was a reluctant prophecy. He had not sought it, or wanted it. Before God came to him in that whirlwind, he had not even thought about religion. He had led an unruly life in his youth and had done many bad things, and felt perhaps that was why he'd been chosen – to demonstrate the mysterious greatness of God.

*

What Walter John Harmon said on this morning was along these lines: Everywhere and at all times, numeration is the same for all mankind. This is because, no less than the earth or the stars, numbers are the expression of God. And so as they add and subtract and divide and multiply, as they combine and separate and conclude, they are the same always to the understanding of human beings no matter who we are or what language we speak. God in the form of numerical truth will weigh the fruit on the scale, He will measure your height, He will give you the tolerances of your engine parts and tell you the length of your journey. He will offer you numbers to go on forever without end, and we call this infinity, because our mathematics count up to God. And when Jesus the Son of God died for our sins, he took to himself the infinity of them because he was of God and could die for the sins of the dead and the living and the unborn for generations to come.

A prophet is not the Son of God, he is one of you, he is an ordinary man of remorse, like you, and so his numbers are no more infinite than the years of his life are infinite. He cannot die for mankind's sins. He may only work to remove the sin of this or that soul, taking it into himself and adding it into himself. Whatever faults you in the eyes of God – your carnal desires, your greed, your attachment to what is unworthy – your mortal prophet lifts from you and takes unto himself. And he does that until the weight of the numbers will bury him and he is welcomed in Hell. For he is an ordinary mortal and if he takes on your sins they become his own and it is to Hell he will go – not to

God at His right hand but to the Devil in the depths of Hell's eternal torment. "Only the adults purified by this prophecy will join the virgin children in the Holy City to come," Walter John Harmon said. 'And I will not be among them."

There was consternation at those words. We knew because the Transference of Sin was the key to his teaching that Walter risked exclusion from the Holy City. We had discussed it at our Meetings. The prophecy was Jesus-like but not Jesus, it was Moses-like but not Moses. Yet to hear it put in mathematical terms was shocking – people stood and cried out, because now Walter John Harmon was speaking of something as incontestable as a sum, as measurable as a weight or a volume, and the reality of such a cut-and-dried formulation seemed almost too much for us to bear.

He did not walk away but looked over us with a faint smile on his lips. Was he suggesting that his doom was imminent? His blond and graying hair was tied this morning into a ponytail, which made him seem younger than his thirty-seven years. And at this moment his pale blue eyes were those of a youth unaware of the tragedy of his life. As he stood and waited, the members were slowly calmed by his silence. We went to him, and knelt, and kissed his robe. Perhaps I was the only one this day to feel that his words were a personal communication. They seemed to be responding to my torments, as if, having intuited my reluctance to seek his counsel, Walter John Harmon had chosen this way to remind me of his truth and to restore the strength of my conviction. But that was the effect always, after all, for the power of his word was in its uncanny precise application to whatever had been in your own mind though you might not have before realized it.

All who heard him this day knew the truth of his prophecy and the resolution and peace of surrendering to it. I felt once again the privilege of the Seven Attainments. I loved Walter John Harmon. How then could I fault my wife's love for him?

A week or so later I dressed for the outer world and drove one of our SUVs to the state courthouse in Granger, a trip of some sixty miles. Whenever I walked into a courthouse now, I felt a great unease, as an alien in a strange land. Yet I had passed the bar exams of three contiguous states and had spent my adult life in the general practice of law and so there was simultaneously a professional sense of belonging to such buildings as this old red stone horror with its corner cupolas, which dominated the square at the city's center. It spoke to me as the native architecture of my own American past, and when I climbed the worn steps and heard my heels clicking on the floor of the entry hall, I had to remind myself that I was an envoy from the future, about to address in their own vocabulary the denizens of the dark ages of secular life.

This was to be a hearing before an administrative judge. The state commissioner of education had moved to suspend the Community's license to school its children. A failure to comply with the statutes requiring mandatory literacy for every child was said to be grounds for a suspension. We were met not in a courtroom but in a room used mostly for jury empaneling in tort cases. It had big windows and dark-green shades pulled against the morning sun. The state had a trio of lawyers. The judge sat behind another table. There were chairs around the walls for spectators – all filled. As far as I knew there had been no public announcement of this morning's hearing. A couple of policemen stood by the doors.

The state argued that in using only the Book of Revelation to teach our children to read and write, and further, that in permitting them ever after to read nothing else than the Book of Revelation, or write nothing but from its passages, we were in default of the literacy statutes. The distinction was made as between education and indoctrination and that the latter as practiced by our cult (I rose to object to that derogatory label) contravened the presumption of literacy as a continuing process, generating ever-widening reading experiences and access to information. Whereas in our close-ended pedagogy, when one text and one text only was all the child was going to read, or recite, or intone, or chant forever after, the open-ended presumption of literacy was negated. The child would learn the text by heart and by rote repeat it with no further call on linguistic skills.

I argued that literacy had no such open-ended presumption, it merely meant the ability to read – that when the state's own inspectors had sat in on our first- and second-grade classes they were satisfied that the principles of reading and writing were being taught in terms of word recognition and phonetics, spelling and grammar, and that it was only when they had discovered, in the upper grades, that the Book of Revelation was the children's sole reading material that they found the Community at fault. Yet the children as taught by us are in fact able to read anything and are literate. Because we direct their reading and contemplation to the sacred text that is the basis of our beliefs and social organization, the commissioner would impinge on our right of free religious expression as set forth in the First Amendment. Every religion teaches its tenets from one generation to the next, I said. And every parent has the right to raise his child according to his beliefs. That is what the parents of our Community were doing and had every right to do, whereas the claim of failed literacy was on the face of it an attempt to interfere with a minority's religious practice of which the commissioner does not approve.

The judge ordered a suspension of our license but declared at the same time that, the issues being substantive, he would defer his order so as to allow time for a court challenge. It was what I expected. The lawyers and I shook hands and that was it.

But as I was leaving the room one of the spectators stopped me, an older man with gnarled hands and a cane.

You are working for the Devil, sir, he said. Shame on you, shame, he called after me. And then in the corridor a reporter I recognized was at my side, walking with me at my pace. Playing the freedom-of-religion card, eh, counselor? You know they'll really be down on you now. Studies, tests, videotapes, school records. Process of discovery.

Nice to see you, I said.

Anyway, you bought yourself six months. Six more months of doing what you do. Except of course if your boy is nailed before then.

Christ was nailed, I said.

Yeah, the reporter said, but not for having a Swiss bank account.

I was relieved to get back to the great valley as a soldier is relieved to get back to his own lines. There was a lovely sense of bustling anticipation as the weekend approached: We were to have an Embrace.

This was a once-a-month occasion when we received outsiders who had heard of us, and made inquiries, or had perhaps attended one of Walter John Harmon's outside Meetings and found themselves interested enough to spend the day with us. They parked their cars at the Gate and were brought up by hay wagon. In our early days we didn't think of security. Now we copied down driver's licenses and asked for signatures and names of family members.

On this Saturday morning in May perhaps two dozen people arrived, many with children, and we greeted them with heartfelt smiles and coffee and cake under the two oak trees. I was not on the Hospitality Squad, but Betty was. She knew how to make people feel comfortable. She was pretty and compassionate, and altogether irresistible, as I well knew. She could immediately spot the most needful tender souls and go right to them. Of course, no one who appeared on these days was not needful or they wouldn't have come. But some were skittish or melancholic or so on the edge of despair as to be rudely skeptical.

In the end, no one could withstand the warmth and friendliness of our Embrace. We treated all newcomers like long-lost friends. And there was plenty to keep everyone busy. There was the tour of the residences and the main house, where the children put on a sing. And there was the Enrobing. All the guests were given the muslin robe to wear over their clothes. This had the effect of delighting them as a game would delight them, but it also acclimated them to our appearance. We didn't seem so strange then. Several long refectory tables were brought out from the carpentry shop and the guests helped lay the cloths and carry out the bowls and platters with all the wonderful foodstuffs – the meat pies, the vegetables from our gardens, the breads from our bakery, the pitchers of cool well water and the homemade lemonade. All the children sat down together at their tables and all the adults at theirs, there in the warm sun. Every guest was placed between two members with another directly across. And our Elder Sherman Beasley stood, who had a naturally booming voice, and he said grace, and everyone tucked in.

It was such a beautiful day. I was able to sit in my place at the end of one of the long tables and to forget for a while the threats to our existence and to feel blessed to be here under a blue sky and to feel the sun on my face as God's warmth.

The conversation was lively. We were instructed to try to answer every question as diplomatically as possible. We were not to give doctrine or theology – only the Elders were entrusted to do that.

A shy young woman on my right asked me why she had not seen any dogs in our Community. She was physically unprepossessing, with thick glasses, and she held herself on the bench as if to take up as little space as possible. This is sort of like a big farm, she said in her thin voice, and I've never been on a farm that didn't have a dog or two.

I told her only that dogs were unclean.

She nodded and thought awhile and after a sip of lemonade, she said: Everyone here is so happy.

Do you find that odd?

Yes, sort of.

I couldn't help smiling. We are with Walter John Harmon, I said.


After lunch came our big surprise. We took everyone to the West Section, where on a prelaid cement base a house was going up for a recently sworn in couple. The framing was done and now as everyone sat in the grass and watched, we men arose and, under the guidance of our carpenters, some of us went to work on the board-and-batten siding, others were up on the roof beams, laying out the planking, and the skilled among us were fitting out the doors and the windows. Of course none of the inside finishing would be done that day, but the thrill our guests had was in seeing so many of us making such quick work of building a home. It was a lesson without words. In fact it was a kind of per-formance because we had built the identical home many times over and each man knew what he had to do and where each nail went. There was a natural music to all the hammering and sawing and hauling and grunting and we could hear our audience laugh and occasionally applaud with delight.

At the end, as we all stood by, Elder Manfred Jackson presented a scroll to the new first-floor occupants, the Donaldsons, a gray-haired couple who held hands and wept. After the Donaldsons were embraced by several members and brought to sit down among them, Elder Jackson turned to the visitors and explained what they had witnessed: They had witnessed the Third Attainment.

Manfred Jackson was our only black Elder. He was an imposing figure, tall, his shoulders as squared as a young man's though he was in his eighties. His hair was white and he wore the muslin robe like a king. With the Third Attainment, he said, these communicants of the Unfolding Revelation have forsworn all their personal property and given their wealth to the prophet. The Third Attainment is a considerable step up, for it is no small matter to abjure the false values of the world and rise from its filth. The prophet teaches us there are seven steps to God-worthiness. Ours will be the kingdom of the chaste and the absolved, because whatever is ours, whatever we possess, whatever we think we cannot do without, we give to the prophet as his burden. He has brought us to live apart from the clamor and lies of the unbelieving. We wear his muslin to declare ourselves in transit. We live in homes to be blown away in the tornado of God. Manfred Jackson pointed out over the valley where the Holy City would descend: We wait upon the glory that needs no sun, he said.


All this time Walter John Harmon had not been seen. As the day went on, heads turned this way and that as our guests wondered where was the man who had drawn them here in the first place. By mid-afternoon all the organized events, the choir recital, the walking tour of the sacred land, and so on, were concluded, and the visitors began to think of leaving. We had collected their muslin robes as if to give them leave to depart. They were indecisive. Some of their children were still playing with ours. The parents were looking for someone to make the first move toward the hay wagons. In the meantime we Elders and members continued to walk with them and express pleasure at their coming, gradually drifting with them back toward the Tabernacle. We knew what to expect, but we let them discover for themselves the prophet sitting quietly there beside the wood table. A child saw him first and called out, and it was the children who ran ahead, their parents following, and a murmur of awe went through them as they slowly gathered in the grass and looked upon Walter John Harmon.

This was always a thrilling moment for me, a culmination of the day's Embrace. See? I wanted to call out, do you see? a great surge of pride filling my breast.

The prophet's custom was to speak to the visitors, but this day he was lost in thought. His eyes were lowered. He sat slightly forward in the chair, one ankle tucked behind the other and his hands folded in his lap. His feet were bare. People settled down in the grass, waiting for him to speak, and even the children grew quiet. More and more members joined us, and there was absolute silence. The ground was cool. The light of the afternoon sun was beginning to throw shadows and a small breeze blew across the grass and played in the hair of the prophet. Betty was suddenly beside me, dropping to her knees, and she took my hand and squeezed it.

Minutes passed. He said nothing. The silence passed the point of our uneasiness or expectation and became significant. A great peace entered me and I listened to the breeze as if it were a language, as if it were the language of the prophet. When a cloud passed over the sun I saw the moving shadow on the ground as his writing. It was as if his silence was transmuted to the language of the pure world of God. It said all would be well. It said suffering would cease. It said our hearts would be healed.

As the silence went on, it became so unendurably beautiful that people began to weep. Someone stepped past me and went to the prophet as he sat there in his impassive loneliness. It was one of the visitors, a chubby blond child who couldn't have been more than fifteen or sixteen. She lay down before Walter John Harmon, and curling herself into a fetal position, she touched her forehead to his feet.

Six families among the visitors that day would pledge to the non-residential tithing that is the First Attainment. But as our Community continued to grow, in a kind of perverse linkage, the attentions of a vindictive world were growing, too. Unfortunately, one of the registrants at the Embrace was a columnist from a Denver newspaper, who must have gotten in under an assumed identity. She described the events of the day accurately enough – such was her craftiness – but the tone of the piece was condescending, if not contemptuous. I could not understand why a columnist would want to come all the way from Denver to sneer at us. The column was not libelous in the legal sense, but I felt personally betrayed when I recognized from the columnist's photo the unprepossessing young woman with thick glasses who had sat next to me at the midday luncheon and asked me how everyone could be so happy. How underhanded she had been, and with such animosity in her mousy being.

At a steering committee meeting, the Elders Imperatived

that the monthly Embraces should thenceforth be limited to families with children. I thought, given the needful of this world, that such a restriction was unfortunate, but the fact was that we were beginning to feel embattled. Allegations that we were all familiar with, having heard them many times over, were regularly communicated to us – by relatives, friends, or professional contacts on the outside – as if we had to be enlightened: *Your prophet is an alcoholic. He abandoned a wife and child. He has grown rich at your expense.* How could any of this have been news to us inasmuch as our prophet was what, in our entirety, we had been? As Walter John Harmon took our evil unto himself, we had emerged newborn, with our addictions, our concupiscence, and our depthless greed lifted from us.

His life was no secret. Every moment of it was a confession. But as the outer world was as darkly inverted as the negative of a photograph, so was its logic.

Each instance of negative publicity seemed to encourage another suit or investigation of one kind or another. Elder Rafael Altman, our CPA, informed us one morning that the IRS had applied for a court order to subpoena the Community books. One of our lawyers was dispatched to apply for an injunction. Those others of us with skills still practiced on the outside met in extraordinary session with the Elders to come up with some overall strategy for dealing with an increasingly impinging world. As to bad publicity, up to this point we had met all of it with a pious silence. Now we decided for the prophet's sake that we must speak out on his behalf, we must give witness. We would not proselytize, but we would respond. Judson Berglund, a high Attainist who before coming to us had run his own public-relations firm in California, had the Imperative to organize this effort. He quickly brought order. When a national newsweekly questioned the miracle of the Fremont, Kansas, tornado, Berglund saw to it that they printed Elders' testimony in their letters to the editor. An attack by a well-known anticultist we boldly duplicated on our Web site, along with the countervailing responses of dozens of our members. And so on.

It only became us, though, to respond to everything patiently, resolutely, and in the spirit of forgiveness.

Walter John Harmon was typically stoic about all the problems mounting up, but as the summer drew to an end and the leaves of the oak trees began to turn, he seemed more and more withdrawn, as on that day of the Embrace. He seemed irritated that nothing he did went unnoticed, as if our devotedness was pressing on him. Yet he was called by God to have no private life, no private feelings, and so we worried about him. Our joyful life of peace and reconciliation, the exultant knowledge infused in all our beings of an exquisite righteousness in the sight of God, and the prayerful anticipation of the coming to our green earth of God's Holy City, was shadowed now by our concern for the spirit of His prophet. When the children sang, he was inattentive. He took long walks alone in the holy site. I wondered if it were possible that the weight of our sins had already become too burdensome for his mortal soul.

*

What I remember now is Walter John Harmon standing with my wife, Betty, in the orchard above the Tabernacle on a chilly gray afternoon in October. Clouds dark with rain sailed through the sky. A wind blew. The orchard trees were only three or four years old, the apple, pear, and peach trees not much higher than a man. Only the apple trees were in fruit now, and on this windy gray day, while Betty's charges ran about picking apples off the ground or reaching for them on the lower branches, I watched Betty hold an apple out to Walter John Harmon. He took her wrist in his hand and leaned forward and bit into the apple she held. Then she took a bite, and they stood looking in each other's eyes as they masticated. Then they embraced and their robes, whipped by the wind, clung to their shapes, and I heard the children laughing and saw them running in circles around my wife and Walter John Harmon in their embrace.

Some mornings after this, members who had gone to pray noticed a robe lying on the ground beside the Tabernacle table. It was his, the prophet's. We knew that because, for ceremonial occasions, he wore not muslin but linen. Now it lay as if he had dropped it at his feet and walked away. The latchkey was still on the table, but the white stone was on the ground. The Elders were quickly summoned to study the scene. Carpenters placed stanchions around the site so that the gathering members would not disturb anything.

Efforts were made to locate Walter John Harmon. We had never ventured past his front door. This was now found to be open. Inside, the place was a shambles. Empty liquor bottles, broken dishes. His closet was empty. Down at the Gate, someone reported that the Hummer was gone.

At noon, with all work stopped, the Elders announced to the stunned Community that Walter John Harmon was no longer among us. There was absolute silence. Elder Bob Bruce said the Elders would convene shortly to make a determination as to the meaning of the prophet's disappearance. He led us in prayer and then urged everyone to go back to their tasks. The teachers were to take their children back to their classrooms. As everyone dispersed, one group of children stood where they were, there being no teacher to lead them. These were Betty's charges. Her puzzled colleagues took the children in hand. Everyone was distracted, unsettled.

I could have told them all the prophet was gone when, the night before, I heard Betty rise from her bed, dress, and slip out the door. I listened, and in a while, in the darkness, I heard through the clear cold night the distant sound of an engine turning over, revving up.


When it was discovered that the prophet had left with my wife, I was called before the Elders. I was invited to join them in their councils. Perhaps they believed the cuckolded husband was enlightened as they were not. Perhaps they thought he was important in other ways. Surely the challenge to no member's faith could have been greater than the challenge to mine, and if I could forbear and sing the praises of God, who would not sing with me?

Whatever their reasoning, I took solace in their dispensation. My personal grief was subsumed. For the sake of my sanity I wanted to find resolution and strength from this crisis. But I also understood quite clearly and unemotionally that were I to think of Betty's betrayal with a forgiving spirit and concentrate on its larger meaning, I would both ease my heart and put myself forward in the minds of the Elders as an exemplar of our Ideals. In a community such as ours one's moral currency might someday be exchanged for an executive role.

The discussion went on for three days. I spoke with increasing confidence and have to admit I had no small part in the deliberations. We came to the following consensus: Walter John Harmon had done what was both required and foreordained by the nature of his prophecy. Not only had he forsaken us who had loved him and depended upon him, but by running off with one of the purified wives, he had cast doubt upon the central tenet of his teaching. What further proof did we need of the truth of his prophecy than his total immersion in sin and disgrace? It was thrilling. Elder Al Samuels, a tiny, bent-over octogenarian with the piping, scratched voice of the very old, was also the most philosophically inclined. He said we were confronted with the beautiful paradox of a prophecy fulfilling itself by means of its negation. Elder Fred Sanders, known and loved for his ebullience, stood up and

2  am was prepared

shouted, Glory be to God for our blessed prophet! We all stood and shouted, Hallelujah!

But while all of this was being worked out, the Community had languished. There was a good deal of crying and wandering about listlessly on the part of many. People could not do their work. Extra prayer sessions were called but went sparsely attended. And a few of the members, poor souls, even packed their meager belongings and walked down the road to the Gate, heedless of all pleas. I think that is how word got out about our situation – through our dispirited defectors. It did not help that a TV news broadcast showed a picture of the Community from a helicopter flying over us while an announcer spoke of us as collectively duped, robbed of our estates, and left humiliated and penniless in the middle of nowhere.

It was time to act. On the advice of Judson Berglund, who had so far managed our public relations effectively, a great celebration was prepared, with music from our string musicians and tables of good food and a goodly supply of our ceremonial wine. Work and school were suspended for the people of the Community to gather and be together. Thanks be to God, the weather softened into one of those October days when the sun, low in the sky, casts a golden patina over the land. Yet the sense of irresolution, of bewilderment, did not entirely lift. People wanted to hear the Elders. I noticed that some of the children had sought out their natural parents and now clung to them.

After lunch, the musicians retired and everyone gathered before the Tabernacle. The Seven Elders arranged themselves on wooden chairs facing the assemblage. One by one, they rose to speak. Their pronouncement was along the following lines: The prophet had all but warned us this would come to pass. He said he would not be among the blessed who would reside in the Holy City. That he has gone so soon is a stunning blow to those of us who loved him, as we all loved him, but we must love him more now that he has done this thing. That is our Imperative. We cannot question what he has done, for it is nothing else but his final sacrifice. He has taken into himself all the sins of the world that we had accumulated and returned with them to the world that we might be made righteous in the eyes of God. Nor should we mourn him: If we live as we have lived, and learn as we have learned, wherever he is will he not still be in our midst? For this reason, from this day forward we Elders will speak in his voice. We will say his saying and think his thinking. And the prophecy that was is the prophecy that is. For he has cast the stone down and the key is here on the table that will open up the door to the Kingdom of God. And when the four horsemen come riding over the land and the plagues rise like a miasma from the earth and the sun turns black and the moon blood-red, and when firestorms engulf whole cities and the nuclear warriors of the world consume one another, the prophet shall be with us and in the carnage and devastation we will be untouched. For God came to earth one day as a tornado, as a whirlwind that spun around this humble man, whose goodness and moral stature only God could see to be His prophet. And we who are your Elders saw it with our own eyes. And we tell you when God comes down again, He will not be a whirlwind, He will be the resplendent self-illuminating city of His glory and His peace, and we who have lived to the prophecy of Walter John Harmon will walk down these pastures and reside there forever.

The Elders were effective. I could see resolution firming up in the postures and facial expressions of the members. Many glances were sent my way. I found myself basking in the reflected glory of my faithless wife, who had been chosen by Walter John Harmon to join him in the ultimate sin, his betrayal of the Community.

A day or two later, when one of the women went into the prophet's house to clean it up, she noticed something under a chair that had been overlooked in the excitement: a pencil.

Our prophet had never wanted anything written.

The Elder who was summoned discovered something else: In the fireplace, half buried in the ashes, were three sheets of paper that had curled and were slightly charred on the edges but were still, miraculously, intact.

On these pages Walter John Harmon had laid out plans for a wall to be built around our Community. He'd provided sketches and measurements. The Gate down by the highway was to be drawn back to just one hundred and ten yards from our buildings. The wall was to be of stone, three cubits thick and four cubits high. The stones were to be gathered from the pasture and from brooks and streams. They were to be bonded with a cement mixture whose proportions he had carefully indicated. And then, a cryptic sentence written at the bottom of the last page of instructions added to the mystery: This wall for when the time comes, is what it said.

Clearly, this was a discovery of unsettling magnitude. It brought forth only questions. A wall of stone did not accord with the Ideal of impermanence that had guided all our previous construction. What did that mean? Did it amount to a new Ideal? And when would what time come? But he had thrown the plans into the fire. Why?

We simply didn't know what to do about these plans. Had they not been discarded, almost certainly they would constitute a Demand.

The pages were preserved in a clear plastic folder and put in the safe of the business office pending further study.

In the meantime, we had to sort out our overall situation. We had been left with very little operating capital. All surrendered estates of members were made liquid through a succession of trusts and routinely placed in the prophet's name in several numbered Swiss bank accounts to protect against legal incursion. He had personally dispensed sums as they were applied for by our financial Elder, Rafael Altman. We grew our own food and clothed ourselves humbly, but we were in arrears for the material costs of our building program, which had gone on more or less continuously as new members arrived. Perhaps we would not have that many more new members for a while. But several of our parcels of valley land for the descent of the Holy City were heavily mortgaged. And were we to lose even one of the standing civil suits against us, we would be terribly vulnerable.

As the weeks went by, it became apparent we faced a long cold winter of untold hardship. Our infirmary, with its one doctor and two nurses, tended to a host of ailing children. There were a number of cases of flu. Elder Al Samuels succumbed to pneumonia and we buried him in the rise behind the orchard. The little bent-over man with the piping voice was well loved and the fact that he was almost ninety when he passed was no consolation to the Community. My own sadness was only slightly appeased when the surviving Elders elevated me to their company. We need younger blood, Elder Sanders said to me as he gripped my arm. Our witness is passed to you by decree.


It is now January of the New Year and I write secretly at night in the privacy of my house. Perhaps, as the prophet says, the time for documentation comes only when the world overtakes us. So be it. This has not to do with a loss of faith – mine is strong and does not give way. My belief in Walter John Harmon and the truth of his prophecy does not falter. Yes, I say to the skeptics: It is entirely unlikely that someone as uneducated and hapless and imperfect as this simple garage mechanic can have designed such an inspired worship. And only the sacred touch of God upon his brow can explain it.

The Community as it huddles on these snowy plains is smaller, but by that fact tighter and more resolute, and we gather each morning to thank God for our joyous discovery of Him. But the world is overwhelming, and if we do not survive, at least this testimony, and others that may be written, will guide future generations to our faith.

Given the general age and infirmity of the Elders, I now function as the managing partner functions in a law office. And Walter John Harmon has come to live through me and will speak in my voice. I have studied the three pages of his plans and I have made the decision that in the first days of thaw we will send our people out to the holy pastures to collect the rocks and boulders for our wall. And one of the newer members, a retired army colonel to whom I've given the plans, has gone out and paced the land. He says it is amazing that our prophet has no military experience. For, as designed, these breastworks take every advantage of the terrain and give us positions for a devastating enfilade.

We are assured of a clear and unimpeded field of fire.

# CHILD, DEAD, IN THE
# ROSE GARDEN

Special Agent B. W. Molloy, now retired, tells the following story: One morning the body of a child was found in the Rose Garden. The sun had just risen. A concert had been given the night before in celebration of the National Arts and Humanities Awards, an event held every year in May. The body was discovered by Frank Calabrese, sixty, the groundskeeper, who had arrived in advance of his workers to oversee the striking of the performance tent. Dew was on the grass and the air was fresh. The light inside the tent was soft and filled with shadows. What Calabrese saw under two folding chairs in a middle row at the east end of the tent was a small Nike running shoe protruding from a shroud-like wrapping. Not knowing what else to do, he phoned the Marine guard post.

In a matter of moments the on-duty Secret Service were at the site. They secured it and radioed the FBI. At the same time the President was awakened, the measures for emergency evacuation of the White House were put in motion, and in short order he, separately, and his family, their overnight guests, and the resident staff were away from the area.

The shroud was scanned and then unwrapped by the FBI bomb squad. The body was that of a boy, white, perhaps five or six years old. It bore no explosives. It was photographed, covered again, put in a plastic bag, and taken away in the trunk of an unmarked Agency sedan.

After the public rooms of the White House and the grounds had been gone over, the President's party was allowed to return. The workers who had been held with their truck outside the gates were waved in and a few hours later all trappings of the ceremony of the night before had been removed and the White House grounds and gardens stood immaculate under the mid-morning sun.

At seven-thirty that same morning Agent Molloy, a twenty-four-year veteran of the Bureau, who worked in the Criminal Investigation Division, met with the chief of the Washington field office. You're the SAC on this one, his chief said. Whatever you need. I don't have to tell you – they are livid up there.

And so, just a few months from retirement, Molloy found himself the agent in charge of a top-priority case. It didn't matter that the event was without apparent consequences. There was no place in the world with tighter security than the White House complex, and someone had breached it – someone who seemingly could carry a dead child wrapped in a sheet past all manner of human and electronic surveillance.

He had delicate issues to deal with. He wanted first of all to have all military and Secret Service personnel on duty the night before account for their actions. He wanted everything diagrammed. The agents he assigned this task looked at each other and then at him. I know, I know, Molloy said. They have their routines, we have ours. Go.

From the White House social secretary Molloy procured the list of the previous night's guests. Three hundred and fifty people had been invited to the evening's concert – awardees, their families, their publishers, dealers and producers, cultural figures, Washington A-list culls, members of Congress. Then there were the orchestra players, various suppliers, and press. Maybe as many as five hundred names and SS numbers to check. He called his chief and got the manpower. Dossiers, if any, were to be pulled. He hoped research would reduce the need for interrogations to a fraction of the attendees.

With everything up and running, Molloy had the groundskeeper brought to his office. Calabrese was a simple man and somewhat stunned by the high-powered reaction to his discovery. He had been in government service all his working life and had years of White House clearances. He was a widower who lived alone. He had a married daughter, a lawyer, who worked in the Treasury Department.

I just seen this sneaker, he said. I didn't touch a thing. Not the chairs. Nothing.

Were the chairs moved?

Moved?

Out of line.

No, no – they was straight. And this sneaker sticking out. It was a kid, wasn't it? A dead kid.

Who told you?

Nobody had to tell me. Imagine. And all wrapped around in white, like a cocoon. That's what it reminded me. A cocoon.

Calabrese had nothing more to offer. Molloy told him he was not to speak of the matter to anyone, and had already sent him out to await a lift back to the White House when a call came from one Peter Herrick, a White House deputy assistant secretary in the Office of Domestic Policy, saying the groundskeeper was to be detained incommunicado under provisions of the counterterrorist statutes until such time as all investigative questions had been answered to the President's satisfaction. A formal authorization would be coming shortly from the Attorney General's office.

The gall rose in Molloy's throat. In my judgment that is a mistake, he said.

We've got to put a lid on this, Herrick said. Nobody other than the President knows the reason for this morning's alert. If this is in the nature of a terrorist act of some kind, it should not be given air.

Without a doubt, Molloy said. But when Calabrese is reported missing, we'll end up answering more questions than we want to. His daughter's a lawyer in Treasury.

I'll get back to you, Herrick said.

Molloy says that only when the line went dead did it occur to him to wonder why the White House liaison re this matter was the Office of Domestic Policy.


At noon he heard from Forensics. The boy had been dead from forty-eight to sixty hours. There were no signs of abuse, no grievous injuries – death was from natural causes.

Molloy went to the lab to see for himself: The body was supine, its hands clenched at its side. Attached to a lanyard around its neck was a bronchodilator. The mouth was open. The face was florid. The eyelids did not completely cover the bulging eyes. The little chest was expanded, as if the kid was pretending to be Charles Atlas. He had black hair a bit longer than it should have been. Molloy had the impression he might be Hispanic.

No foul play here, the pathologist said. You're looking at respiratory failure. The airways spasmed and closed up.

From what?

Kid had asthma. The worst kind – status asthmaticus. Comes a time when no inflammatories or dilators can control it. To keep him breathing, because he can't get rid of the carbon dioxide, he would have to be put on a respirator. I guess where he was, there was none available.

The boy's clothing had been sealed in plastic bags: T shirt, jeans, briefs. Gap items. No nametags. Together with the shroud, and the Nikes, the clothing was still being analyzed.

151

He hoped for something, he didn't know what. Maybe a lot identification that would indicate origin of shipment.

At eight the next morning, Molloy went back to the Rose Garden and stood looking at the White House from where the orchestra platform had been. Fifty feet away and somewhat to the side was a staked ribbon to show the body's position. He wondered when a wrapped body could have been brought into the tent so that it would not be noticed by any one of hundreds of people until the groundskeeper came to work the following morning. Conceivably, it could have been brought in after the concert was concluded and everyone had left and the lights were turned off – but that was a scenario he didn't want to think about. It meant he would need to direct his investigation to persons who would not have been required to leave the premises once the evening was over.

Over the next several days considerable manpower was used in an attempt to identify the child. Once they knew who he was, the question of who had brought him onto White House grounds would begin to answer itself. In the meantime, the agents called him P.K., for Posthumous Kid. With photos in hand, they checked missing-children files, visited hospital pediatric wards, and interviewed pulmonologists in D.C., Virginia, and Maryland. No leads were forthcoming. The Bureau's national data bank showed no reported kidnappings to match his description. As the paper piled up on Molloy's desk, he remembers he wondered at what point these inquiries, which were bound to create gossip, would come to the attention of someone whose profession it was to ask questions.

In order to comply with directives calling for inter-agency cooperation, Molloy held a briefing for a deputy of the Secret Service, an electronic-security expert assigned to the NSA, and a psychologist consultant to the CIA whose specialty was terrorist modalities.

Molloy didn't know any of them. I don't have much time, he said, and quickly filled them in.

Secret Service sat tall in his chair, a man in his late thir-ties, early forties who obviously used the gym, his suit as if tailored to his musculature. Well, he said with an icy smile, are we clean?

So far, Molloy said.

The electronics man with the NSA said he could run a system check, but the system was self-monitoring. It sends out an EKG that would have shown something, he said. So we'd already know.

Molloy's own techs had told him the same thing.

The psychologist held his chin in his hand and frowned. Would you say this was a symbolic action, Agent Molloy?

I'd say.

I remind you that 9/11 was strongly symbolic, in case you think what we have here is necessarily over and done. You might be tempted to invoke the sixties as historical precedent, when you had those anti-nuke activists tres-passing government property and pouring blood on missile housing and so on. Where they were more interested in propagandizing than doing real damage. But you would be wrong. Those hippie types were American. They put their bodies on the line. They took jail terms. They didn't sneak in, leave their calling card, and sneak out. So this is something else entirely. Something more ominous.

Like what, Molloy said.

Like a warning. As in, We've done this so you see we can.

So a dead boy doesn't mean anything in particular? Molloy said. He's just a calling card?

Well, they brought him from somewhere, the consultant said. This feels to me like an Arab thing.

Secret Service said, Still no I.D.?

No.

Nothing ethnic?

No. A white kid. He could be anything.

Then he could be from where they hate us, the psychologist said. He could be a Muslim kid.


In the second week of the investigation, a break came when a district commander of the D.C. police, John Felsheimer, called Molloy and invited him for an after-hours beer. The two men had worked together on occasion over the years, and while they were not exactly friends, they had a high regard for each other's professionalism. That they were of the same generation, family men with grandchildren, was another bond between them.

Once they'd exchanged amenities, Felsheimer withdrew

a letter from his breast pocket. He said he was sorry he had not learned of the FBI investigation of a missing person until he happened to pick up some scuttlebutt that very day. He said the letter had been left at his district station a week before. Unsigned, undated, it was a single page, with just one computer-typed sentence. "You should know that a child was found, dead, in the Rose Garden."

Felsheimer explained that Molloy was holding a Xerox copy – the original had been kept by the White House. He had put the original in a glassine envelope and taken it to the office that liaised with the D.C. police. Rather hastily, he'd been shunted over to the Office of Domestic Policy, which he thought odd. A deputy assistant, a Peter Herrick, had heard him out and expressed surprise that he, Felsheimer, would attach any importance to a crank letter. But then Herrick had said he would hold on to it.

Felsheimer, on his second beer, recalled the conversation:

So you're saying there was nothing in the Rose Garden?

No, I didn't say that, Commander Felsheimer. What it was, was an animal.

An animal?

Yes. A raccoon. FBI did the tests. It died of rabies. It just came in there to die.

We don't see much rabies in Federal City.

Well, you live and learn. Just to be safe, we had the First Dog tested, checked the kids of staff, and so on. Negativo problems. It just wandered in and died. End of story.

So, Brian, Felsheimer said to Agent Molloy after a

pause. Am I wrong to put two and two together? Is that why the FBI is into missing-persons work now? You're looking to make an I.D. on a dead kid?

Molloy thought awhile. Then he nodded yes.

And the kid was found where the letter said?

Molloy said: John, for both our sakes, I have to ask for your word. This is a classified matter.

Felsheimer drew another letter from his pocket. Of course you have my word, Brian. But you may be glad you leveled with me. Here's a letter that came this morning addressed to the district commander, meaning me. When I heard you were running the show, I knew better than to go back to the White House.

This letter text was exactly the same as the first. Computer-printed, Times Roman, fourteen-point. And unsigned. But unlike the first letter, it had come through the mail. And the envelope had a Houston postmark.


Molloy did not blame himself for assuming, from the lab report of time of death – forty-eight to sixty hours before the body was examined – that the child had lived and been treated in D.C. or Virginia or Maryland. He put in a call to the chief of the FBI field office in Houston, whom he had known since their days as agent trainees, and asked for the complete paid obituary notices in all the Texas papers for the month of May. And throw in Louisiana, Molloy said.

Naturally, knowing you, the chief said, I'm to put this at the top of my things-to-do list.

You got that right, Molloy said.

He called his secretary into his office and told her to run the National Arts and Humanities Awards guest roster through the computer to tag all names with Texas addresses. The names as of today? she said. It's down to under a hundred. The original list, Molloy told her.

He sat back in his chair and considered the mind of the person or persons he was dealing with. They had wanted it made public. Why then had the press not been tipped off? Why wasn't it now a rumor flying all over the Internet? Only a note delivered to a district station and, upon a lack of response, a note mailed, this time almost as a reminder to the district commander? How peculiar to rely on authority when authority is what had been subverted. But there was something else, something else . . . a presumption that a line could be drawn between those powers who might be trustworthy, like local police, and those who were thought not to be, like himself. It did not square with the boldness of this bizarre act that the person who committed it had a hopeful regard for the law. Molloy had from the beginning theorized that he was dealing with eco-terrorists. But he had now the scintillating sense of a presiding amateurism in the affair.

It was time for a meeting with the White House liaison, Peter Herrick. Molloy found a balding blond young man who wore Turnbull & Asser shirts with french cuffs. Herrick had been a hotshot regional director in the last campaign, a President's man. Molloy had seen his like over the years. They came and went but, as if it were a genetic thing, always managed a degree of condescension for federal employees putting in their time.

You heard from John Felsheimer, Molloy said.

Who?

D.C. police. You took a piece of evidence from him.

I suppose so.

I'll have it now, Molloy said.

Just sit down, Agent Molloy. There are things you don't know.

Withholding evidence is a chargeable offense, even for White House personnel.

Perhaps I was overprotective. I'll dig it up for you. But you appreciate why we can't have any leaks. It would be like the other party to jump on this for political advantage. There's so little else they have going. And this is the kind of weird shit that sticks in the public's mind.

What things don't I know?

What?

You said there were things I don't know.

No, I was speaking generally about the political situation. I wonder why we haven't heard your working hypothesis. I assume you have one? Wouldn't you think it figures, from this crowd, something disgusting like this? The desecration of a beloved piece of ground? Not that I ever expect the artists, the writers, to show gratitude to the country they live in. They're all knee-jerk anti-Americans.

You let a hypothesis limit an investigation and you can get off on the wrong track, Molloy said.

I'm thinking of the cases musical instruments come in. That kid could have fit into a cello case, a tuba.

The program was Stephen Foster and George Gershwin, Molloy said. There are no tubas in Stephen Foster or George Gershwin.

I used that as an example.

The cases are left back at the hotel. The instruments are examined on the bus.

Writers were on hand whose books are adversarial to the Republic. Painters of pictures you wouldn't want your children to see. Our reward for these socialist giveaway programs.

Molloy rose. I do admire your thinking, Deputy Assistant Secretary of Domestic Policy Herrick. You have any more helpful ideas, pass them on to my office. Meanwhile, I'll expect that letter.


Molloy knew that as a piece of evidence, the letter was useless. It would be dime-store stationery, just like the one in his possession, and overhandled at that. But he had to make a point. This group trusted only themselves. Molloy was certainly no liberal, but he detested politically driven interference in a case.

He was put in a better mood that same afternoon when one of his agents brought him a missing-persons bulletin taken from the interstate police net: Frank Calabrese, widower, age sixty. The report had been filed by Ann Calabrese-Cole, his daughter. Molloy smiled and told his secretary that when a call came from the Office of Domestic Policy, she was to say he was out.

He now had dossiers – some thirty of the guests had files. He set to work. A while later he looked up and noticed that the windows of his office had grown dark. He turned on his desk light and kept reading, but with a growing sense of dissatisfaction: There were book publishers and art dealers who'd marched against the Vietnam War. A playwright who'd met with a visiting Soviet writers' delegation in 1980. University teachers who'd refused to sign loyalty oaths. Contributors to the Southern Christian Leadership Conference. A lawyer who'd defended priests in the Sanctuary movement. A professor of Near Eastern studies at George Mason. A folksinger who'd gotten an arts award several years before . . . He knew only halfway through the pile that it was useless, as if he could hear the voice that had written *You should know that a child was found dead in the Rose Garden.* It was not the voice of any of these files. These were the files of people, who, no matter for what cause, were by nature self-assertive. What he heard here was a circumspect voice going quietly about an unpleasant duty. It sounded to him like a woman.

Molloy was handed a FedExed 250 MB Zip disk from Houston when he arrived at work the next morning. He gave it to a young agent nerd whom he suspected somewhere down the line of having considered a career in criminal hacking. Would have done quite well, too: In an hour the nerd produced published notices for every child twelve and under who had died in every city and county in Texas and Louisiana in the month of May, then a refined list by city and county of male child deaths in south Texas and southwest Louisiana, and, under that, a target list of all young male deaths in south Texas and southwest Louisiana that had occurred within seventy-two hours of the ceremonial in the Rose Garden.

Molloy sighed and started in on the target list. He first looked for the age and struck out names of kids over seven. Then he eliminated names that to his mind connoted black children. With the names remaining, he read in detail the simply worded expressions of heartbreak: beloved son of . . . alive in our hearts . . . classmate of . . . taken from us . . . in the bosom of Jesus . . . It was not with any sense of satisfaction, but with something like a disappointment in himself, that he came upon what he knew he had been looking for. In the Beauregard, Texas, *Daily Record* a boy named Roberto Guzman, age six, had been remembered in three paid obits – by his parents, by his cub scout troop, and, crucially, by someone unidentified, who had written "Rest in Peace, Roberto Guzman, it was not God who did this to you."

Molloy told his secretary to make out the appropriate travel forms and book a next-day flight to Houston with a car rental at the airport. He had a pile of paperwork to go through – the agent interviews were still coming in – but he thought he'd have another look at the cadaver. He seemed to remember there was a small brown mole on the kid's cheek. The on-site flash photos weren't any good. He requisitioned a Sony Cyber-shot and went off to the morgue.

The kid was not there.

Molloy, stunned, questioned the attendant, who knew nothing about it. Wasn't on my shift, the attendant said.

Well, someone took it. You people keep a book, don't you? Bodies just don't fly in and out of here.

Be my guest.

Molloy found nothing written to indicate a child's body had been received or taken away.

Immediately, he called his bureau chief. He was told to come right over.


Now, what I'm about to tell you, Brian, his chief said – you have to understand a policy decision has been made that was explained to the director, and however reluctantly, he has chosen to go along.

What policy decision?

The investigation is concluded.

Right. Where's the kid? I'm pretty sure I've made an I.D.

But you're not listening. There is no kid. There was no body in the Rose Garden. It never happened.

So where'd they bury him?

Where? Where they would not be questioned, where nobody would see them at two in the morning.

The two men looked at each other.

They panicked, the chief said.

Did they, now?

They shouldn't have detained that groundskeeper who found the body.

You're so right.

Someone tipped his daughter over in Treasury. So they swore him to secrecy, sprung him, and allowed as they'd been holding him as a material witness on some classified matter. But they also told her that they'd perceived signs of dementia. So if he does say something –

That's really low.

It wasn't just that. The *Post* is nosing around. Someone sent them a letter.

From Texas.

Well, yes. How did you know?

I can tell you what it said, Molloy said.


When Agent Molloy got back to his office, he was seething. He sat down at his desk and, with his forearm, swept the stack of paperwork to the floor. There'd been a pattern of obstruction from the start. He'd felt an operative intelligence in the shadows all through this business. On the one hand they wanted answers, as why wouldn't they, given an intolerable breach of security? On the other hand they didn't. They may have made their own investigation – or they may have known from the beginning. Known what? And it was so sensitive it had to be covered up?

Whenever Molloy needed to cool off, he went for a walk. He remembers how, when he first came to Washington as a young trainee, he'd been moved almost to tears by the majesty of the nation's capital. Quickly enough it became mere background to his life, accepted, hardly noticed. But in his eyes now it was the strangest urban landscape he had ever seen. Classical, white, and monumentalized, it looked like no other American city. It was someone's fantasy of august government. On most any day of the week, out-of-town innocents abounded on the Mall. The believers. The governed. He kept to the federal business streets, where the ranks of dark windows between the columns of the long pedimented buildings suggested a nation's business that was beyond the comprehension of ordinary citizens.

Back in his office, Molloy scrambled around on the floor looking for the awards-ceremony guest list. When he found it, it was as he'd thought – no Texas residents. At this point it occurred to him that if the President had had personal friends staying over that night, they might not have been on this list. Personal friends were big-time party supporters, early investors in the presidential career, and prestigious moneyed members of his social set. They were put up on the second floor, in the Lincoln Bedroom or across the hall in the suite for visiting royalty, these friends.

Molloy left a message with the White House social secretary. By the end of the day his call had not been
returned. This told him he might not be crazy. Like everyone else in Washington, he knew the names of the in
crowd. A couple of them had cabinet appointments,
others had been given ambassadorships, so they were not
possibles. But one or two of perhaps the most important
held portfolios as presidential cronies.

On a hunch, he called the controllers' tower at Dulles.
He would have to show himself with his FBI credentials to
get the information, but he thought he'd give them a head
start: Molloy wanted to know of any charter or private air-
craft logged out of Dulles with a flight plan for anywhere
in Texas the morning after the awards event.

In heavy rush hour traffic he drove to the airport. He
was tired and irritable. His wife would be sitting home
waiting for him to appear for dinner, too inured to the life
after all these years even to feel reproachful. But his spirits
lifted when an amiable controller in a white shirt and rep
tie handed him a very short list. Just one plane matched his
inquiry: a DC-8 owned by the Utilicon Corporation, the
Southwest power company, with home offices in
Beauregard, Texas.

He had some leave time coming and put in for it and flew
to Houston on his own money. Looking down at the
clouds, he wondered why. Over the years he'd been

involved in more than his share of headline cases. But in the past year or two he'd felt his official self beginning to wear away – the identity conferred by his badge, his commendations, the respect of his peers, the excitement of being in on things, and, he had to admit, that peculiar sense of superiority as a tested member of an elite, courteous, neatly dressed, and sometimes murderous police agency. In his early days he would bristle when the FBI was criticized in the press; he was more judicious now, less defensive. He thought all of this was his instinctive preparation for retirement.

How would he feel when it was over? Had he wasted his life attaching himself to an institution? Was he one of those men who could not have functioned unattached? He had suspected of some of his colleagues that they had taken on the federal agent's life as much for their own protection as anyone else's. Whatever his motives, it was a fact that he'd spent his life contending with deviant behavior, and only occasionally wondering if some of it was not justifiable.

He picked up a car at the airport. Beauregard was about an hour's drive to the east. He could see it miles away by the ochre cast of sky.

At the outskirts, he turned off the interstate and continued on a four-lane past petrochemical plants, oil storage tanks, and hardscrabble lots that were once rice paddies.

The Beauregard downtown looked as if it had succeeded in separating itself from the surrounding countryside: a core of glass-curtain office buildings, a couple of preserved old brick hotels with the state flag flying, chain department stores, and, dominating everything else, the skyscraping Utilicon building, a triangular tower faced in mirrors.

Molloy did not stop there but went on through the residential neighborhoods where imported trees shaded the lawns, until, after crossing the railroad tracks, he was bumping along on broken down roads past bodegas and laundromats and packed-dirt playgrounds and cottages with chain-link fences bordering the yards.

He pulled over at the Iglesia de la Bendida Virgen. It was a clapboard church, unusual for Catholics. The priest, Father Mendoza, a younger man than Molloy, slender, with a salt-and-pepper beard, explained that it had been built by German immigrants in the nineteenth century. Their descendants live in gated communities now, he said with a wry smile.

They sat in the shade on the rectory porch.

You realize I can say nothing.

I understand, Molloy said.

But yes, Juan and Rita Guzman are my congregants. They are righteous people, a virtuous family. Hardworking, strong.

I need to talk to them.

That may be difficult. They are being detained. Perhaps you can tell me what exactly is the motivation of the INS.

I have no idea. That is not my bailiwick.

I will tell you the child had last rites. A mass. Everything from that point to burial a scrupulous celebration of the Mystery.

Molloy waited.

Unfortunately, in the shock of bereavement, in the sorrow of their loss, people are at their weakest, the father told him. Sometimes the consolations of the Church and the assurance of Christ do not quite reach to the depths of the heart of even the most fervent believer. Are you a Catholic, Mr. Molloy?

Not as much as I used to be.

This is a poor congregation, the priest said. Working people who just get by, if that. They love their Blessed Virgin. But they are learning to be Americans.

The Guzman bungalow was like any other on the street, except for the little front yard – it was not burnt-out, it was green. It had hedges for a fence and a carefully tended border of the kind of wildflowers that Mrs. Johnson, the former First Lady, had once designated for the medians of Texas highways.

The inside of the house was dark, the shades drawn. A stout old woman in black and a girl of about twelve watched Molloy as he looked around.

In the sitting room, a boy's grade-school photo was the centerpiece of a makeshift shrine on a corner table: Roberto Guzman in life, with a big smile and a little brown mole on his cheek. The picture was propped against a bowl of flowers placed between two candles. On the wall behind it was a carved wooden crucifix.

Molloy glanced at the girl: his older sister, with the same large dark eyes but without Roberto's deep shadows underneath.

Special Agent Molloy with the image of the dead boy in his mind felt the shame of someone who had seen something he shouldn't have. He mumbled his condolences.

The old woman said something in Spanish.

The girl said: My grandmamma says, Where is her Juan? Where is her son?

I don't know, Molloy said.

The old woman spoke again and shook her fist. The girl remonstrated with her.

What does she say?

She is stupid, I hate her when she is like this.

The girl began to cry: She says the Devil came to us as a señorita and took my mama and papa to hell.

The two of them, the old woman and the girl, were both crying now.

Molloy went through the little kitchen and opened the back door. There in the hazy sun was a formal garden with brick-edged flowerbeds, shrubs, small sculpted trees, grass as perfect as a putting green, and a small rock pool. It was very beautiful, a composition.

The girl had followed him.

Molloy said, Is Señor Guzman a gardener?

Yes, for Mr. Stevens.

Stevens, the chairman of the power company?

What is the power company?

Utilicon.

*Sí*, of course the Utilicon, the girl said, tears running down her cheeks.

Before he left, he took down a phone number from a pad beside the wall phone: in faded ink, *el médico*.

He found the Beauregard City Library and read Glenn Stevens's c.v. in *Who's Who*. It was a long entry. Utilicon's nuclear and coal plants provided power for five states. Molloy was more interested in the personal data: Stevens, sixty-three, was a widower. He had sired one child, a daughter. Christina.

Molloy got into his car and drove to the Stevens estate and was admitted by a gatekeeper. Several hundred yards down a winding driveway were the front steps.

I thought this was all settled, Glenn Stevens said as he strode into the room. Molloy stood. The man was well over six feet. He had graying blond hair combed in pompadour style, a ruddy complexion, and a deep voice. He wore white ducks and a pale yellow cashmere sweater and loafers with no socks.

Just tidying up some loose ends, Molloy said. He had waited twenty minutes to be received. The Stevens library was paneled in walnut. Settings of big leather chairs, polished refectory tables with the major papers and magazines laid out in neat rows. The french windows opened onto a deep stone terrace with potted trees and balusters wound with white flattened flowers.

But the books in the scantily stocked shelves – the Durants' *Story of Philosophy*, the collected works of Winston Churchill, Richard Nixon memoirs, Henry Kissinger memoirs, and ancient best-sellers in Book-of-the-Month-Club editions – were not up to scratch.

I didn't know the Bureau was involved, Stevens said. Nobody told me that. Molloy was about to reply when a young man in pinstripes and carrying a briefcase came into the room. As fast as I could, he said, mopping his brow.

I thought I'd better have counsel present, Glenn Stevens said, and sat down in a leather armchair.

Our concern is we were told the Bureau had been called off.

That's true, Molloy said. The incident is not only closed, it never happened.

You have to understand that Mr. Stevens would never embarrass the President, whom he admires as no other man. Or do anything to bring disrepute to the great office he holds.

I do understand.

Mr. Stevens was one of the President's earliest supporters. But more than that, the two men are old friends. The President regards Mr. Stevens almost as a brother.

I can understand that too, Molloy said.

And he has shown the tact and grace and compassion so typical of him in assuring Mr. Stevens that nothing of consequence has happened and that their relationship is unchanged.

Molloy nodded.

So why are you here? the lawyer said.

This is a family matter, Stevens chimed in. And while it may be extremely painful for me personally, it is only that, and if the President understands, why can't the damn FBI?

Mr. Stevens, Molloy said, we do understand that this is a family matter. It has been judged as such and sealed. Nobody is building a case here. But you must understand a serious breach of security occurred that calls into question not only the Bureau's methods but the Secret Service's as well. We have to see that such a thing never occurs again, because next time it may not be a family matter. We would not be fulfilling our mission were we to be as casual about the President's safety as the President.

So what do you want?

I would like to interview Miss Christina Stevens.

Absolutely not, Mr. Stevens! the lawyer said.

Sir, we're not interested in her motives, the whys or wherefores. Molloy flashed an ingratiating smile and continued: But she pulled something off that I, as a professional, have to admire. I just want to know how she did it, how this young woman all by herself managed to leave egg on the faces of the best in the business. I know it's been difficult for you, but considering it purely as a feat, it was quite something, wouldn't you say?

She betrayed my trust, Stevens said hoarsely.

Mr. Stevens means his daughter is not well, the lawyer said.

Look, sir, sure she did. But there will be an internal investigation of our procedures. And I'm sure you appreciate how it is with company men – we have to cover our ass.

Out on the gravel driveway at the bottom of the steps the lawyer gave Molloy his card. Anything else, from now on, you deal with me direct. No more unscheduled visits, Agent Molloy, agreed?

Where is this place?

Do you know Houston?

Not very well.

When you get there, give them a call and they'll lead you in. It's no mystery, you know.

What is?

How she did it. One look at Chrissie Stevens and you'll understand.

The lawyer was smiling as he drove off.

Molloy stayed that night at the Houston Marriott, eating room service and watching CNN. He liked the bureau chief here but didn't want to have to answer for himself. What he did was put in a call to Washington – a lady friend from his bachelor days, a style writer for the *Post*, who had since moved up in marital increments to her present life as a Georgetown power hostess.

The gal has quite a history, Molloy. Isn't this a little late for your midlife crisis?

You'll be discreet, I know, Molloy said.

Chrissie Stevens is a flake. She was riding pillion with a Hell's Angel at the age of fourteen. Then she found religion, Zen wouldn't you know, and spent a couple of years in Katmandu in some filthy ashram. Oh, and she lived in Milan for a year with some Italian polo player till she dumped him, or he dumped her. You want more?

Please.

Not just once has she been in for detox at Betty Ford. That's the talk, anyway. You know my theory?

Tell me.

Lives to pay Daddy back for the life he's provided her. I mean, that may be her true passion – they are really a very intense couple, Glenn and his daughter Chrissie. But you know what's most remarkable?

No.

You sit across from her at the dinner table and she is spectacular. A vestal virgin, not a sign of wear and tear. Brian, she has the most beautiful skin you can imagine, coloring I would die for. Goes to show.


The phone number Molloy had found in the Guzman kitchen was for the office of a Dr. Leighton, a pulmonologist, one of three associates in a clinic a few blocks from the Texas General medical complex. The waiting room was packed, aluminum walkers and strollers abounding: women with children on their laps, the elderly, both black and white, clutching their inhalators. Three TV sets hung from the walls. Eyes were cast upward – a chorus of labored breathing and bawling children blocked out the sound. It was a world of eyes sunk in hollow sockets.

A nurse, turning pale at the sight of Molloy's credentials, had him wait in an examining room. Molloy sat in a side chair next to a white metal cabinet on which sat racks of vials, boxes of plastic gloves. On the facing wall, a four-color laminated diagram of the human lungs and bronchia. In a corner, on the other side of the examining table, a boxy looking machine hung with a flexible tube and mask. Nothing out of place, everything immaculate.

Dr. Leighton came in, equally immaculate in his white coat over a blue shirt and tie. He was a bit stiff, but quite composed and professorial-looking behind wire-framed glasses. He leaned back against a windowsill and with his arms folded looked as fresh as if he had not been tending all morning to an office full of people who had trouble catching their breath. Molloy remarked on the crowd.

Yes, well, the smog has been worse than usual. You put enough nitrogen oxide into a summer day and the phones light up.

I wanted to ask you about the Guzman boy who died last week, Molloy said. I understand he was your patient.

Am I obligated to talk with you?

175

No, sir. Do you know a Christina or Chrissie Stevens?

The doctor thought a moment. A sigh. What would you like me to say – what is it you want to hear? The boy suffered terribly. On days like this, he was not allowed to go to school. He tried so hard to be brave, to control his terror, as if it was unmanly. He was a great kid. The more scared he was, the more he tried to smile. In this last attack, they rushed him up here – Chrissie and the priest and the boy's father – and I put him on intubation. I couldn't reverse it. He died on me. Roberto didn't need a respirator, he needed another planet.

Chrissie Stevens had been checked in to the Helmut Eisley Institute, a sanitarium for the very wealthy.

Molloy found her in the large, sunny lounge to the right of the entrance hall. She was seated on a sofa, her legs tucked under her, her sandals on the carpet. He had not expected someone this petite. She was the size of a pre-teen, a boyishly slim young woman with straight blond hair parted in the middle. Her elbow propped on the sofa arm, her chin resting on her hand, she was posed as if thinking about Molloy as she stared at him.

But don't you people travel in twos? she said with a languid smile.

Not all the time, Molloy said.

Behind her, standing in attendance, was a very young Marine in olive drab too warm for the climate. He had the flat-top haircut, the ramrod posture, the rows of ribbons, of a recruitment poster.

This is my friend Corporal Tom Furman.

When the corporal put his hand on her shoulder, she reached back and covered his hand.

Tom is visiting. He just flew in today.

Where are you stationed, son?

When he didn't answer, Chrissie Stevens said, You can tell him. Go ahead – nothing's going to happen. It's been decided.

Sir, I'm posted at the White House.

Well, Molloy said, that's a plum assignment. Does it come with the luck of the draw or is it saved for the very exceptional?

Sir, yes. We're chosen I suppose, sir.

Ah me, ah me, Chrissie Stevens said. Can we all sit down, please? Pull up a chair for Agent Molloy and you sit beside me here, she said to the Marine as she patted the sofa cushion.

And so the two men sat as directed. Molloy hadn't anticipated Chrissie Stevens as a Southern belle. But she was very much that. His own daughters, straightforward field-hockey types, would have taken an instant dislike to her.

She was strikingly attractive, very pale, with high cheek-bones and gray eyes. But what was mesmeric was her voice. That was where the vestal-virgin effect came from. She had a child's soft Southern lilt, and when she lowered her eyes, her long blond lashes falling like a veil over them, it was as if she had to examine in her mind the things she was saying to make sure they were correct, and the effect of an ethereal modesty was complete.

I'm not here of my own volition, Agent Molloy. Apparently I've done something for which the only possible explanation is that I've gone off the deep end. But if that is true, what other questions are left to ask?

I have just a few.

Though it's not at all bad here, she said, turning to the corporal. They fatten you up and give you a pill that makes you not care about anything much. They stand there until they see you swallow it. I'm out to pasture right now. Are my words slurred? I mean, why not, why not, you can dream your life away, she said with her sad smile. That's not so bad, is it?

Molloy said: Did you know that the boy's parents are faced with deportation?

Clearly, she didn't.

But I think that can be stopped, he said. I think there's a way to see that it doesn't happen.

She was silent. Then she mumbled something that he couldn't hear.

I beg your pardon?

Deport me, Agent Molloy. Send me anywhere. Send me to Devil's Island. I'm ready. I want nothing more to do with this place. I mean, why here rather than anywhere else? It's all the same, it's all horribly awful.

Molloy waited.

Oh Lord, she said, they always win, don't they. They are very skillful. It didn't come out quite as we planned – we are such amateurs – but even if it had, I suppose they would have known how to handle it. I just thought maybe this could restore them, put them back among us. It would be a kind of shock treatment if they felt the connection, for even just a moment, that this had something to do with them, the gentlemen who run things? That's all I wanted. What redemption for little Chrissie if she could put a tincture of shame into their hearts. Of course I know they didn't give our gardener's son the asthma he was born with. And after all they didn't force his family to live where the air smells like burning tires. And I know Daddy and his exalted friends are not in their personal nature violent and would never lift a hand against a child. But, you see, they are configured gentlemen. Am I wrong to want to include you, Agent Molloy? Are you not one of the configured gentlemen?

Configured in what way?

Configured to win. And fuck all else.

Her Marine reached over and held her hand.

What do you think? Chrissie Stevens said. Am I making sense? Or am I the family disgrace my father says I am?

The both of them were looking at Molloy now. They made a handsome couple.

Would you like some refreshment, Agent Molloy? There's a bell over there – they bring tea.


Back at his desk in Washington, Molloy caught up on the cases that he'd left when the call came in about the dead child in the Rose Garden. One of the cases, a possible racketeering indictment, was really hot, but as he sat there he found his mind wandering. His office was a glass-partitioned cubicle. It looked out on the central office of lined-up desks where the secretaries and less senior agents worked away. There was a nice hum of energy coming through to him as phones rang and people went briskly about their business, but Molloy couldn't avoid feeling that he was looking at a roomful of children. Certainly everyone out there was at least twenty years younger. Younger, leaner, less tired.

This is what he did: He put in a call to Peter Herrick at the Office of Domestic Policy and quietly told him, though not in so many words, that if the parents of the dead child were not released by the INS and allowed to return home, he, Molloy, would see to it that the entire incident became known to every American who watched television or read a newspaper.

Molloy then sat at his computer and composed a letter of resignation.

The last thing he did before he turned out the lights and went home to his wife was to write, by hand, a letter to Roberto Guzman's parents. He said in the letter that Roberto's grave might be unmarked but that he rested in peace at the Arlington National Cemetery among others who had died for their country.